MW01124730

The Impatient Dissidents

A New Sherlock Holmes Mystery

Note to Readers:

Your enjoyment of this new Sherlock Holmes mystery will be enhanced by re-reading the original story that inspired this one –

The Adventure of the Resident Patient.

It has been appended and may be found in the back portion of this book.

The Impatient Dissidents

A New Sherlock Holmes Mystery #23

Craig Stephen Copland

Published by:

Conservative Growth Inc.
3104 30th Avenue, Suite 427
Vernon, British Columbia, Canada
V1T 9M9

Cover design by Rita Toews.
ISBN-13: 978-1546797821
ISBN-10: 1546797823

Dedication

To those individuals and members of their families who suffer from Post Dramatic Stress Disorder, a tragedy that was present in the days of Sherlock Holmes and is still with us.

Welcome to New Sherlock Holmes Mysteries -

"The best-selling series of new Sherlock Holmes stories. All faithful to The Canon."

Each story is a tribute to one of the sixty original stories about the world's most famous detective. If you are encountering these new stories for the first time, start with *Studying Scarlet,* and keep going. (https://www.amazon.com/dp/B07CW3C9YZ)

If you subscribe to Kindle Unlimited, then you can 'borrow for free' every one of the books.

They are all available as ebooks, paperbacks, hardcovers, and in large print.

Check them out at www.SherlockHolmesMysteries.com.

NEW SHERLOCK HOLMES MYSTERIES

WWW.SHERLOCKHOLMESMYSTERY.COM

Contents

Acknowledgments

All writers of Sherlock Holmes fan fiction or pastiche stories are indebted to the genius of Sir Arthur Conan Doyle or, for the true Sherlockians, to Dr. John Watson, for the creation of the sixty original stories, the Canon, of Sherlock Holmes.

In all the stories I write, I drop quotes and references to many other books, movies, events, and works of art. Hope you enjoy spotting them.

My dearest and closest friend, Mary Engelking, not only encourages the continued writing of these stories but for this story also provided corrections to my use of words from the Russian language.

Several wonderful and invaluable fans of Sherlock Holmes have kindly offered their services as Beta readers and provided exceptionally worthwhile comments, suggestions, and corrections. I extend my gratitude to them yet again.

During the recent past, I have finally become active on Facebook and joined the community of social media Sherlockians. Their continued informational and celebratory posts about Sherlock Holmes and Arthur Conan Doyle are enriching my enjoyment of the quest more and more. Thank you.

Chapter One

From Russia, Without Love

He morning of the fourteenth of March, 1881 is seared into my memory.

It began as an inauspicious Monday morning in 221B Baker Street, where Holmes and I had been sharing rooms for a few months. His solving of the crime I later described as *A Study in Scarlet* had concluded, but no new adventures had overtaken us. Our parsimonious life was not particularly exciting, and we were not far from the clutches of the mendicancy squad. I was struggling to establish my medical practice and Holmes spent much of his day at his chemistry table, trying to make effective use of his time whilst waiting for a client to arrive and present him with a case.

I rose early that day, bathed and dressed, and entered our front room. I could hear a bit of a commotion down on the pavement and, my curiosity aroused, I peered out our bay window to the street below. Although it was still quite early, there were three newsboys there and all were surrounded by a crowd of Londoners eagerly snatching the morning papers from their hands and then stepping back to read the story on the front page.

I was still a young man in those days but my time in the wars asserted itself on my leg and my attempt to bound down our seventeen steps several at a time was not my most graceful performance. I rushed out to the street, tuppence in hand, and bought a paper from the nearest lad. The headline was a mere two words:

CZAR ASSASSINATED

I walked slowly back up the stairs, reading as I did so. The first few paragraphs informed the readers that in St. Petersburg, on the previous morning, Czar Alexander II had traveled from his palace for his weekly inspection of the troops. Whilst his carriage was being driven along the embankment of the Catherine Canal, an anarchist, a member of the *Narodnaya Volya* or People's Will movement, had hurled a bomb under his carriage. It exploded, killing one of his guards and injuring several pedestrians, but the Czar himself had been spared. Tragically, he got out of his carriage to inspect the damage and whilst he was standing on the pavement, another anarchist rolled a bomb under the horses and towards the Czar. The explosion had torn off the Emperor's lower legs, cut into his stomach and lacerated his face. He died soon afterward.

Having served on the front lines of a battlefront, I had seen my share of arms and legs blown asunder and shrapnel and scrap metal cutting into men's bodies. And yet I was horrified. The English people had been given the impression that Czar Alexander was "The Liberator" who had freed the serfs and was slowly bringing Russia into the modern age. The Russian people were about to get some sort of a parliament for the first time in their history. Supposedly, the Czar was popular with his subjects. We English believed that the unspeakable mutilations of war should not happen in one's own country in times of peace. Clearly, that sentiment did not extend to the Russians.

Sherlock Holmes was sitting at the breakfast table when I entered our rooms. I laid the newspaper in front of him and he leaned over and read the story. When he had finished, he slowly looked up at me, shaking his head.

"The times are out of joint," he said. "O cursed spite. An event like this is only the beginning. In ages past the people would cry 'The king is dead. Long live the king.' But now the cry has become 'We want it now!' These dissidents and anarchists are foolishly impatient. They hastily create chaos, but only more chaos and trials and tribulations come to pass."

"The report," I noted, "said that the killers had been captured straight away and their partners in crime were being rounded up. Do you not think that will put a stop to it?"

"No, my friend, sadly, I do not. These movements are like the Lernaean Hydra. You cut off one head, and another two grow in its place. Yesterday morning was only the calling card.

More horrors are on their way. Once the cauldron of unrest boils over, it cannot be stopped."

Holmes returned to reading the newspaper, and I hustled to get ready to see my patients. The necessity of giving attention to other demands temporarily pushed the Russian tragedy from my mind. But at the end of the day, whilst I was returning home, I picked up the afternoon paper and read the most recent news that was now being made public. The two anarchists who had hurled the bombs had been identified and were on their way to the gallows, but the members of the movement, now reported to be in the hundreds, had scattered themselves. The respectable London newspapers, what few there were, tried to refrain from hysterics. The tabloids were screaming; *The Russians are Coming!* and *They're on Their Way to England!* and sought to terrify the citizens of London with fanciful accounts of Russian anarchists escaping the clutches of the Russian police and making their way to the East End.

The stories of the events in Russia remained on the front pages for the next several days, but then, as with all news stories, they faded and were replaced by more recent events, as is required if newspapers are to be bought and read. The week following the horrible event in Russia, the war Britain was fighting with the Boers in the Cape came to an end, and three days after that there were riots in Basingstoke as the publicans clashed with the crusading marchers of the Salvation Army. That strange event was eclipsed by the sinking of the ferry, the *Princess Victoria,* in the Thames and the loss of one hundred and eighty lives.

As one news story faded and then another, the horror of the Czar passed. His son, Alexander III, although not yet crowned, took over the reins of power and immediately announced a restricting of freedoms across the vast country and a persecution of all dissidents.

April arrived, the flowers came into bloom and the chaffinches started singing across England and, for a while, I seemed to forget about what had happened and Holmes's ominous warning.

Although I did not perceive it at the time, the truth of his words came to fruition in the first week of June.

Holmes and I had taken a long and leisurely stroll during a pleasant evening and wended our way from Baker Street to the Strand and along Fleet Street. We agreed to work our way back home via Kensington and take a look at the newly opened, magnificent Natural History Museum.

An announcement was posted on the building's notice board stating that a brilliant young medical researcher from King's College Hospital, Dr. Percy Trevelyan, was going to be giving a lecture. I knew of this chap. He was a graduate of London University, as was I, and had recently published a much-praised monograph in *The Lancet* on catalepsy and affective disorders. His lecture, scheduled for the following morning, bore the title: *New Treatments for the Alleviation of Soldier's Heart with Specific Reference to the Employment of the Extracts of Certain Narcotic Plants.*

"You might enjoy it," said Holmes, as he read the announcement. "Do you know this fellow?"

"He was several classes in front of me," I said. "But I certainly know who he is. Quite the impressive young scholar. So, yes, I would enjoy it. I shall plan on attending."

From Kensington, we strolled back north through the park and on to Speakers' Corner, chatting as we went.

"I assume," said Holmes, "that you have observed this disorder they are calling 'Soldier's Heart' in some of your patients."

"Time and time again," I said. "I saw it first on the battlefield and then treating veterans at St. Bart's. Now, hardly a week goes by without some poor chap coming in, or being brought in by his wife or family. It is as if the war never ended for them. All it takes is the sound of a gunshot, or someone shouting too loud, or sometimes just the sight of blood and they react frightfully. Their heartbeats quicken sharply, their pupils dilate, their hands and lips start to tremble, and their ability to think and speak clearly is diminished. During the night, many of them cry out in terror as they re-live the horrors of the battlefield. Some of the spells are short and mild, and some can last an hour or more and leave the poor chaps mentally and physically exhausted. Very few of them can sustain gainful employment. If this doctor has found any way at all to alleviate the attacks, I would be highly interested."

"Then you must attend," said Holmes, "and do bring me a full report."

I was nearly an hour early for the lecture, determined to get a choice seat near the front. The grand central hall of the recently opened building was gleaming with polished granite and glass and held signs pointing to the exhibits and collections for which it was already famous. A couple of hundred chairs had been set out in front of the great staircase and a dais raised on which the lecturer could stand and deliver his presentation. I took a seat in the second row along the center aisle, knowing that it would afford me both clear sight and sound. As the crowd gathered, I recognized several of my university professors, many old London schoolmen, and a few distinguished members of the Royal Society. Obviously, Percy Trevelyan was on his way to making a mark in the field of medical research. I confess that I felt quite chuffed knowing that neither he and nor I were from the stuffed shirts of Oxford and Cambridge. I rather liked this chap even before I met him.

The lecture itself was polished, confidently delivered, and backed up with impressive research. Dr. Percy recounted the results of his treating scores of veterans with various naturally occurring substances. Opium, cocaine, cannabis, peyote, and khat had all been administered in controlled doses to men who were in serious distress. All had provided some immediate relief, but several had what are referred to as "side effects" that were not particularly positive. While it was still too early in the testing to offer any final conclusions, there were promising possibilities for continued treatment with khat and cannabis, but some distinct dangers associated with opium and cocaine. When the lecture was over, a genuine and generous round of applause was given, and the president of the Royal Society gave effusive praise. I had a few questions that I wanted to pose to the young scholar and waited around until after he had shaken hands with all of the assembled potentates. I then approached him and introduced myself.

"Are you *the* Dr. John Watson?" he exclaimed.

I was taken aback, as I did not expect that anyone in this crowd would have heard of me, let alone a budding scholar. I mumbled some sort of reply, and he continued, smiling.

"Young John Stamford has told me all about you. You gave splendid and sacrificial service to Queen and country out in Afghanistan. Had a bit of a rough go of it, I hear. But as far as I am concerned, it is brave men like you who should be given medals and citations. We medical eggheads just sit in our laboratories and enjoy the facilities of our great hospitals whilst you chaps are out there risking your lives to save others. It is an honor to meet you, Dr. Watson."

Again, I mumbled an embarrassed response, and he carried on.

"I have a note on my desk to contact you."

"Me? But why?"

"I was hoping, you and I both being London University men and all, that you might help me by introducing me to the strange chap you are living with. You are the only man I have heard of that appears to have access to Mr. Sherlock Holmes. Stamford said that he was a consulting detective, the only one in all of England, and utterly brilliant. Strange, mind you, he said, but brilliant. Could I possibly impose on you to arrange a meeting with him? I would be most grateful."

I was about to say that all anyone needed to do to have a meeting with Sherlock Holmes was to knock on his door, but I bit my tongue and nodded, quite enjoying the small measure of importance that I had acquired.

"I am sure," I said, "that he would be willing to meet you. But might I tell him why you are seeking his services?"

"It's all to do with my work with those poor chaps who are suffering from Soldier's Heart. I have an entire ward of them at King's. They are all in very rough shape, but there is one fellow who simply does not know who he is and we cannot, in spite of trying for the past two weeks, find any kith or kin. The police have just said *sorry*, but they have robberies and murders to attend to. So, when I heard about this Holmes fellow and that a London University man was his closest friend, I thought that contacting you would be the best chance I had for helping this poor patient. We do have some funds available and would be more than willing to pay Mr. Holmes's standard fee. Could you possibly arrange a meeting with him this week?"

I assured him that I could and would and shook his hand and walked quickly back to Baker Street, completely forgetting to ask my questions about khat and cannabis.

"Holmes!" I shouted as I ascended our stairs. "Holmes! Are you here?"

"Good heavens, Watson. You do not have to bellow. I have not gone deaf. Please, be silent, so I can concentrate on this reaction."

"Well then, listen. I have found a case for you. A case with a client who will pay you. Would you like to hear about it, or shall I be silent?"

He extinguished the alcohol lamp and put the test tube in the rack before turning to look at me.

"Speak."

"It might not be the most unusual case you have ever taken on, but there is a chap in King's College Hospital, and neither he nor any of the doctors know who he is. However, they are prepared to hire Sherlock Holmes to solve the mystery."

"Details, please. And do try to restrict yourself to facts and avoid conjecture."

I told him what I had been told and watched as he nodded slowly. A faint smile could be discerned behind his otherwise impassive face.

"The case appears to have some redeeming elements of interest to me. Would you mind sending a note back to your Dr. Trevelyan suggesting that we will meet him tomorrow morning after he has completed his rounds? I assume you will come with me. If a case emerges from the morning, I will need your services as my Boswell."

Although Holmes and I had only been flatmates for a short time, I had come to know him well enough to take such a response as the equivalent of a wildly enthusiastic *Yes!* from an ordinary mortal. I must admit that I even felt a bit smug when I watched him close up his chemicals, stroll over to my shelf of medical books, reach for my copy of the latest compendium concerning mental disorders, and start reading. I was reasonably certain that by the following morning he would have become a minor expert on the affective disorder that doctors had given the name of Soldier's Heart.

Holmes had insisted on an early breakfast and that I bring my leather doctor's case with me. By seven o'clock we were in a cab and on our way across London, past the Lincoln Inn Fields, and to the King's College Hospital on Portugal Street. Upon arriving, we inquired for Dr. Trevelyan and were told that he would still be a half an hour before he had finished his rounds.

"Come, Watson," said Holmes. "Let us redeem the time by making a close study of the establishment."

He did not wait for me to reply but began a slow walk around the exterior of the building and then up and down the corridors. We had a few strange looks from some of the nurses, but as we remained confident and appeared to know where we were going, no one impeded our tour.

At eight o'clock we were met at the entrance by Dr. Trevelyan.

"Thank you for coming, Mr. Holmes. And thank you, Dr. Watson, for making the requisite arrangements. We truly are at our wits' end trying to decide what to do with this poor fellow. Shall I take you to see him?"

I was about to nod in the affirmative when Holmes spoke up.

"Before doing so, might we review his file and ask you some questions about him? I know that you are frightfully busy, doctor, but I will be as succinct as possible and having your insights would be very helpful."

"By all means, ask away."

"Did the man enter the hospital of his own accord or was he brought in? And, if brought to the hospital, who brought him and what was his last known location in London?"

"The police," said the doctor, "brought him in. They picked him up over in Spitalfields Market. A couple of the ladies selling wares in the stalls had seen him walking around as if in a trance and went and found a constable. That was almost two weeks ago."

"Very good, doctor. And has he been interviewed? Does he speak English?"

"Oh, yes. Excellent English. French as well. Now, languages are not my forte, but I could hear a trace of an accent. From the Continent, obviously, and I rather thought from the far side, where all the Slavs live. His countenance also has that look about it. We're calling him *Mr. Smith* as we have no other name for him. Although I suspect he has a foreign name."

"And the condition of his physical health, doctor?" asked Holmes.

"Excellent. His mind has been shattered, but he is a strong and fit man. No symptoms of any malady other than his mental disorder."

"Does he comprehend anything about his situation? How does he respond to your questions?"

"He always answers my questions, quite respectfully. But the answers are confused and inconsistent. He does not appear to remember his name but does recall the names of his parents. Sasha and Maria, he says, although once he called his mother Catherine, but there has been nothing that we could coax from him to locate a family."

"Have you circulated a photograph of him?"

"No, Mr. Holmes and it is understandable that you should ask. It is standard procedure now to have a hospital photographer come in a take a full-face photo and send one of our orderlies over to the neighborhood where an unidentified fellow is thought to live. We do it all the time with corpses that are brought in. But when we brought the photographer into his room, he went into a terrible panic and ended up hiding under the covers. It was so upsetting to him that we have not tried again."

"Ah, that is interesting," said Holmes. "Is he the only case you are caring for now of men with symptoms of Soldier's Heart?"

"Oh, goodness, no. Our doctors see several of them every month. So do the doctors at Ormond, Barts, the Royal, St. Mary's, and everywhere. Many of the patients are not able to be employed, but still quite functional. We only give resident care to those who are in the worst shape and have no family to look after them. We have seven of them in care now. In addition to Mr. Smith, there's one older gent who is a veteran of the war in the Crimea. Two others served in India and battled the Mutiny. There's a young fellow who just got back from the Cape. And then we have a chap who has never been in the Service. He was ten years in the London Fire Department and had a fine record, but then a month ago, he just stopped acting normally and has been a mess ever since. Most of them have symptoms similar to Mr. Smith, but at least we know who they are. A new chap came in just the night before last who is going to be a puzzle. He's hopelessly catatonic. In a complete trance, he is. Not sure how we're going to deal with him."

Holmes carried on for a few more minutes and then, conscious of the demands on the doctor's time, he asked that we be taken to meet the mysterious Mr. Smith.

"My dear Watson," Holmes said to me as we stood outside the room of Mr. Smith. "May I request your assistance here? I will sit in a chair in the corner of the room and appear to be your scribe and as inconspicuous as possible. Could you carry out a thorough physical examination on this fellow as if he were a new patient of yours, and call out what you find and I shall write it down? Would you mind doing that?"

"Not at all."

I did as requested and tested joints, heart, lungs, bowels, hearing, and eyesight and inflicted all those indignant pokes and prods that male patients must endure. The patient clearly understood my requests and moved and adjusted his limbs and body but otherwise said nothing. But all I accomplished was to confirm what Dr. Trevelyan had already told us. The chap was in his mid-to-late thirties and in superb physical condition. He was very muscular and lean and, other than a few scars on his arms and one on his back, he showed no signs at all of ever having suffered any serious malady. He was also rather handsome, in a distinctly Slavic sort of way. It is not an adjective that Anglo-Saxons are accustomed to applying to Slavs and, I assume, the reservation is returned in kind.

Holmes kept writing throughout the examination and, when I had finished, he gestured to me that we should meet in the hallway.

"I believe that I can carry on quite well on my own from here on," he said. "You may as well return to your medical practice. I will stay with this fellow for the rest of the day and through the night. I expect that by tomorrow, or the day after at the latest, I will have discerned his identity."

I had learned that it was no use to ask him how he intended to do whatever he was going to do. Thus, I bade him good-day and took a cab back to Marylebone and my small but growing medical practice.

Chapter Two

Case Opened, Case Closed

H olmes did not return to Baker Street that evening, nor was he present at the breakfast table. It was the late afternoon, after I had completed my doctor's appointments for the day, when I heard the door slam and footsteps quickly ascending the stairs.

"Done," he announced as he swept into the room. "Awfully decent of you to bring me a case but in future, you might try to find one that is not so absurdly simple that a child in nursery school could solve it."

"Really? You mean you found out who the man is? Very well, who is he?"

"His name is Count Ilya Myshkin. Born and raised in the ancient city of Nizhny Novgorod, about four hundred miles east of Moscow at the confluence of the Oka and the Volga, which, by the way, is also the home city of the famous mathematician, Nicolai Ivanovich Lobachevsky, a fact which is not at all significant, and of the writer and radical thinker, German Lopatin, a fact that is.

"He entered the Russian army as a young man, did well and was rapidly promoted. His diligence, along with his strength, military skills, and his good looks, for a Slav, resulted in his being assigned to the elite guard that served the Czar. The folks at the Russian Embassy have been searching for him and were greatly relieved when I reported to them. They will be coming by the hospital tomorrow morning to retrieve him and place him in the care of one of their diplomatic families. I have reported same to Dr. Trevelyan. Case concluded."

He sat down in his chair and withdrew his pipe.

I was astounded. "How in the name of all that is wonderful did you learn that? Did you get the chap to talk?"

"Oh, the details of his life were not terribly difficult to come by. The officials at the Russian Embassy told me all those facts about him. All I had to do was furnish them with particulars of a well-regarded Russian soldier who had been present at the assassination of the Czar, and they immediately knew who I was talking about and told me the rest."

"Holmes, that does not answer my question. How did you find out what you did about him?"

"Elementary, I must confess. I began by pouring a glass of vodka, the universal elixir of the Slavic people, and then asking him a few simple questions along the line of 'What is this object?' and he might reply, 'It is a drinking glass?' and a few more. That permitted me to listen to his accent, which I identified as Russian. As it is not a language in which I have any significant knowledge, I made a quick dash the few blocks to the library at the British Museum and borrowed a basic school text on how to speak Russian. In three hours, I had learned enough for my purposes, and I then asked him a series of questions, the answers to which he would have acquired in his childhood. Almost all major cities in Russia are built on the banks of a sea, lake, or river. I asked the name of the sea closest to his home and received no reply. Next, I tried the river, and he immediately answered, 'The Volga.' Fortunately, the name in Russian is precisely what we call it in English. I then moved to the cities that border the Volga, beginning with Tsaritsyn and worked my way upstream. When I uttered the name of Nizhny Novgorod he eyes blinked in recognition and he replied, 'Ya, Nizhny.'

"It was obvious from his musculature that he was either an athlete or a soldier and his haircut, the scars on his arms and back, and the gleaming polish on his boots all said *soldier*. Now a soldier does not acquire a profound case of Soldier's Heart on the parade square or in a quartermaster's store sorting socks. He acquires it in battle. This fellow is too young to have fought in the Crimean War or in the invasions of Poland or the Baltic States, so that left either the conflicts with Turkey, or with the Mohammedan states of Central Asia. All the native languages of those regions are Turkic, and so I uttered basic military commands in Turkish, such as *sarj etmek!* and *geri cekilmek!* meaning *charge* and *retreat*. Any soldier who had served in those wars would have heard those words, but there was not a glimmer of response. Therefore, I had to wait until the fellow had fallen off to sleep to see if I could get him to give a reflexive response.

"I began by the holding the textbook very close to his ear and snapping it shut. It was a poor imitation of a rifle shot, but it worked. He instinctively shouted out *'Pristreli yego.'* That is Russian for *shoot him.* I snapped the book again, and he shouted the same response but this time added *'Prezhde, chem on uydet'* meaning *before he gets away.* It was not exactly considerate of me, but I closed the door to his room so as not to disturb the nurses and then beat my hands furiously on the side table beside his bed, making as loud a noise as I could all the while shouting *Pomogite! Pomogite!* The poor fellow sat up in his bed and began shouting a stream of Russian phrases in the most anguished voice imaginable. I could not tell clearly what he was saying but I could make out the words for 'bomb' and 'blood' and 'legs' and then, quite clearly 'the Czar.' At that point, I had him. He must have been present at the assassination of the Czar back in March. Seeing and hearing a bomb go off and seeing the Czar with his legs dismembered and the assassin running away and learning of the death of the Emperor he was bound to protect must have completely undone his mind.

"As soon as the morning came, I hastened over to the Russian Embassy and demanded to speak to one of their senior secretaries. At first, I was passed off to a minor functionary, but as soon as I told him that I had information concerning the killing of Czar Alexander, I was ushered into the office of the

First Secretary. I told him that there was a Russian soldier in King's College Hospital who was suffering severe mental distress but that I believed that he had been present at the assassination and that he might, upon recovery, even if temporary, be able to furnish information about the event.

"The Secretary gave a great sigh of relief and thanked me profusely. He told me the chap's name and said that they had been looking for him. He had been staying in the home of a Russian family near Spitalfields and had wandered away. That led me to ask the obvious question as to how it was that a Russian army officer who had been present at the events in St. Petersburg had ended up in London. I had not expected a forthcoming answer, after all, the man was a diplomat and had not reached his rank by speaking the truth, but he surprised me. He said that the fellow, Count Myshkin, was a hero of the Russian people. He had become familiar with the radical writings of German Lopatin as a result of some connection with his family in Nizhny. He had learned all the right slogans to parrot when in the presence of anarchists and had then served as a double agent, infiltrating one of the cells of the People's Way. Unfortunately, he had not been part of the cell that undertook the assassination and had no foreknowledge of the plan. But he knew all the names of those who were the leaders of the movement and gave them to the Okhrana, the Russian secret police. They immediately rounded up as many as they could catch and shot them.

"But some got away and knew that Count Myshkin had betrayed them and were mad as hornets, vowing to do him in. So, he was sent off to London where they believed he would be safe, but the poor fellow was so terribly disturbed by the site of his Emperor being blown apart in front of him that his mind became deranged. He lapsed into what your doctor friends call Soldier's Heart and not only became woefully incompetent but began to go wandering. He was found and delivered to King's College. And so we have it. Next case please."

There was nothing I could say except, "Congratulations. I hope that all your cases are solved so easily."

"That, Watson, is a horrible thing to say. Nothing is so utterly a waste of my time as a case that can be solved in a few hours with minimal mental exertion."

He was in a bit of a blue funk throughout dinner and the rest of the evening and at one point picked up his violin and began to scratch away on it, only to put it away after a few minutes and go to his chemistry table. At half past ten, I left him there and went to bed. I have no idea when he finally went to sleep, but I know exactly when he woke up.

At 6:30 am the next morning there was a loud clanging on our bell from Baker Street. I pulled on my dressing gown and rushed down the stairs. I opened the door and in the early morning light found myself looking into the distraught face of Dr. Percy Trevelyan. His countenance was pale and haggard. He had acquired an unhealthy hue that made it seem as if his strength and youth had been robbed from his soul.

"Doctor Trevelyan," I gasped. "What is it? What is wrong?"

"Is Sherlock Holmes in? Is he up? I must speak with him."

"Please doctor," came Holmes's voice from the top of the stairs. "Come in. I am here and awake at this ungodly hour. What is it?"

Dr. Trevelyan ascended the stairs and walked straight up to Holmes until their faces were only as few inches apart.

"He's dead," he said.

For a minute, Holmes made no reply. "Who? Not the Russian. His mind was shot, but physically he was as healthy as a horse."

"Yes, I know he was. But when I stopped in to see him on my rounds this morning, he was stone cold dead. *Rigor mortis* had already set in. He died sometime around midnight. I immediately called in Doctor Smythe-Harley, the supervising medical officer, and he hastily said that the man must have had a terror attack during the night and that it was such a shock that his heart stopped. He said that there was no need to call the police."

Here he paused and looked directly at Holmes. Simultaneously, both shook their heads.

"I am no doctor," said Holmes, "but I think that highly unlikely."

"Well, I am a doctor, and I think it impossible. So, please, will you come with me back to the hospital?"

Within ten minutes, both Holmes and I were dressed and inside the cab. The streets were still almost empty, and we made fast time getting to the hospital and then up to the ward.

The door to the room occupied by Count Myshkin was closed, but nothing else had been done to indicate that the occupant had died. That was to be expected. We were in a hospital, and people died in their rooms all the time.

Dr. Trevelyan opened the door and led us in. In the bed, lying peacefully on his back, with his eyes closed was Ilya Myshkin. His skin had taken on the pale blue hue of death, but there were no immediate signs of any trauma having been experienced. Holmes walked immediately to the side of the bed close to the man's head and leaned over until his face was almost touching the deceased's. He placed his nose adjacent to the lips and sniffed several times.

"Cyanide," he announced. "It has a distinct smell of almonds and brings death almost immediately without causing vomiting, diarrhea, convulsions, or foaming at the mouth. This man has either ingested cyanide or had it injected into his body by a syringe sometime prior to midnight."

"That is what I feared," said Dr. Trevelyan. "Very well, I will send for Scotland Yard."

He began to leave the room, but Holmes stretched out his hand and placed it on the forearm of the doctor.

"As your supervising medical officer has already claimed that it was mere heart failure, might I beg your indulgence and ask you to postpone calling the police until I have had the opportunity to do a thorough investigation and to question the staff. Once the automatons from the Yard arrive, there will be no possibility to carry out a reasonable study."

The good doctor paused for a moment. "Officially, I should refuse your request, Mr. Holmes, but I think that we could spare an hour, but no more."

Holmes thanked the weary fellow, who then departed. He forthwith drew out his magnifying glass and began an intense examination of Count Myshkin and every object in the room.

"Watson," he said. "Would you mind awfully taking some notes as I call them out to you? A reversal of our roles from yesterday, you might say?"

"Not at all. Ready when you are."

Holmes slowly pulled back the bedding, exposing the powerful torso of the military officer. He first examined the face and neck, looking for the telltale signs of a puncture by a needle. Slowly, he peeled back the pajama shirt, exposing the chest, upper arms, and torso, again looking for the almost undetectable sign.

"Even if the man was mentally undone," I said, "I would suspect that he would have shouted out had someone plunged a syringe into him."

"I suspect the same, Watson. But a competent examination does not depend on what we suspect, only on what we observe to be present or absent. Relying on our suspicions is a certain way to do extremely bad detective work."

He then pulled the blankets and sheets further down until the fellow's mid-section was fully exposed. He smiled and placed the magnifying glass back in his pocket.

"Aha," he said. "No need for further searching for puncture wounds. Here is the murder weapon."

The man's arm was extended beside his body. His hand was still clutching a teacup. Without moving the hand or the cup, Holmes leaned over so as to be as close as possible to the cup.

"Kindly note, Watson, that there is a residue of tea in the cup and the faint scent of almonds. A late evening cup of tea was brought around to him, and the cup he drank from must have had a dose of cyanide dissolved into it. He drank it and died within minutes. A nurse or orderly must have poisoned the tea prior to giving him this specific cup. Watson, would you mind going and finding Dr. Trevelyan and asking him to furnish the names of whatever staff were on duty last night?"

I nodded and departed. King's College is a small hospital, and it was not difficult to track down Dr. Trevelyan. I informed him briefly of what Holmes had discovered and the request to call together the staff who were on duty the previous night so that Holmes could cross-question them.

Dr. Percy Trevelyan looked utterly crestfallen.

"I find it hard to believe that one of our staff could have done such a vile deed. But that appears to be what happened, devastating though it is to think about it. The staff who were on the floor last evening have all gone home now. I shall send notices and drivers to their residences demanding that they return here immediately. But it may take some time to bring them in."

"Perfectly understandable, doctor," I said. "Mr. Holmes and I will wait in your conference room if that is acceptable to you."

"That is acceptable. And please, do not forget, that I cannot put off for much longer sending notice to Scotland Yard. A delay in a matter like this arouses their suspicions, and they become quite exercised about things."

"We will move as fast as we can, doctor," I assured him.

The first staff member to appear before us was a beefy orderly who could have served well in a seething scrum. It was apparent by one look at him that he had been disturbed from a deep sleep and was still not entirely in the land of the awake. We handed him a cup of hot coffee which he first attempted a gulp of and, finding it burned his lips, blew loudly on the edge of the liquid.

"Good morning, sir," said Holmes. "Could you kindly state your name and tell us where you live?"

The chap blinked, blew again on the coffee, and took a sip.

"Me name, right, sir, is 'arold Johnson. I live on Watlin' Street in Cheapside."

"And you were the orderly last night on the west wing of the third floor. Is that correct?"

"Yes sir, that be correct."

"When did you last see the patient known as Mr. Smith, the fellow in room 313?"

"Just before the bloomin' end of me shift, sir. I do a final 'ave a look in ter make sure they were all sleepin' and none in duress, i'n it? That would 'ave been just before two o'clock in the chuffin' mornin', sir."

"Did you notice anything peculiar about Mr. Smith?"

"Peculiar? No. 'e were dead ter the world like the bleedin' rest o' them. Even the crazy ones need their sleep. So, all I do is go in an wisper softly ter spot if they want anyfink. If they say nuffink, then I move on. Wot should I 'ave seen then, sir?"

"You might have seen that he was dead."

The orderly blinked again and stared at us.

"Dead, right, yer say, sir, is it? Well, right, no sir. 'ad I seen that 'e were dead, I would 'ave said sumfink. We 'ave a bit of folks 'ere who die in their sleep. 'Tis not uncommon. But the ones who do are ever right ill or elderly, do wot Guvnor. That Smith chap were as 'ealthy lookin' as they come, i'n it?"

"Indeed, he was. Did you see anyone else on the floor before midnight and up until the time you did your round?"

"Well no, sir. Right. Mainly on account o' I were not on that wing. I also 'ave ter cover the central wing and the chuffin' north wing, and then I come and do the bloody west wing. It's the last one and then I gahn home and make us a nice cup a' tea and go ta bed. So, right, I just came and checked in on the chuffin' patients and went 'ome. There be twenty rooms on a wing. I start wiv number one and work me way up. And there was no one else in sight, except for the bleedin' station nurse at the bleedin' station, wilst I did me rounds, sir."

Holmes paused for several seconds and said nothing. Then he smiled at the orderly.

"Thank you, Mr. Johnson. You have been very helpful, and we do apologize for disturbing your rest. Please, go on home and try to fall back asleep. Good day, sir."

The man raised his bulky body out of the chair, gave both of us a nod, and departed.

The station nurse came in next, and Holmes asked a similar round of questions, but she could shed no light on what might have happened. She was absolutely certain that no one had been on the floor who ought not to have been there. The floor nurse had delivered medications and tea around eleven o'clock. The orderly had been by at two. And the Dr. Trevelyan had started his rounds at six o'clock in the morning.

That left the floor nurse.

"My name is Madelaine Campbell and ah bide on Pine Wynd in Clerkenwell. Bit as ye kin tell, a'm originally a Weegie."

"Yes, miss, I can tell," said Holmes. "And you were the floor nurse last night on the third floor of the west wing."

"Aye, ah wis. Ah bring th' cuppa 'n' medicines tae a' th' doolallies."

"Do you pour the tea, or is it already poured by the staff in the kitchen?"

"Ah pour th' cuppa. Seven cups a' a time. Thare is hee haw worse than a cauld cup o' tay. Ah line thaim up oan mah cart alang wi' th' medicines fur a' th' doolally men."

"And when you have delivered the tea and the medicines to the first seven men, I assume that you pour another seven cups and then bring them to the next lot."

"Aye, that's whit ah dae."

"Did anything unusual happen last night when you brought Mr. Smith his tea? He was the one in Room 313.

"Aye. Th' yin wha is deid, ye mean. No, he wis a gentleman wit manners an all. He complained that it's cuppa tae 'n' nae vodka. Bit he wis joking."

"Ah, so it was an entirely normal night. Nothing unusual.

"Nae we' 313. Bit the jimmy in room 310. He wis a kinch."

Holmes paused and I could tell that some new thoughts had invaded his mind.

"Was he now? In what way?"

"Thay say he is peely-wally in his heid 'n' that is how come he is in his trance. Bit ah kin tell he insae glaikit. Thir's something gaun oan ben his mynd. Ah kin tell, 'n' lest nicht he broke his trance 'n' git crabbit wi' me."

"Did he now? And what did he do?"

"Ah gave him his cuppa 'n' he thro' th' cup agin th' wall. Ah hud tae wash it a' up 'n' sae ah tellt him he wid nae git his cuppa at a' if he acted lik' that agin."

Holmes eyes suddenly widened as if a light had been lit inside his head. He stood quickly.

"Thank you, Miss Campbell. Watson, please come."

I stuffed my pencil and notebook back in my pocket and rushed out behind Holmes. He was almost running up the stairs to the third floor and then stopped at the entrance to the west wing.

"We may have our man," he said. "It is the patient in 310"

Chapter Three

The Russians are Coming

"But he is the fellow who is completely catatonic," I said. "How could he have done anything?"

"A fraudulent imitation, Watson. It is a very easy complaint to imitate. I have done it myself on several occasions. He hears the doctor or the nurse entering and straight away pretends to have gone into his trance. He likely overheard our conversations yesterday. We shall have to surprise him somehow."

We walked quietly down the hall toward room 310. Holmes motioned to me to remove my boots, and I did so, and we approached the door in silence. Then he got down on his hands and knees and began to crawl into the room. I gave a quick glance up and down the hall to make sure that no nurse was watching who might be moved to admit us to the crazies' ward.

We moved slowly and silently. Being low, we were out of the patient's line of sight. Holmes quietly stood up behind the bed, unseen by the fellow, who was placidly reading a book.

"*Dobroye utro. Kak dela,*" he said quietly.

"*Dobroye utro. Ya v poryadke. Spasibo,*" came the reflexive reply.

Suddenly the fellow snapped his head around. He threw the book directly at Holmes's face and leapt out of the bed. I sprang to my feet and grabbed at him, but he smashed a fist into my chin and bolted from the room.

"Catch him! Stop him!" I shouted as I ran after him. A brave little slip of a young nurse stepped out of the nursing station, but he gave her a straight arm, knocked the poor thing over and kept running. I tried running after him, but in my stocking feet I was slipping and sliding all over the polished floor. The madman was in his bare feet and had already entered the staircase a full twenty yards ahead of me. I kept shouting for someone to stop him but the stairwell was empty, and he was soon down to the ground floor and out the door.

I gave chase across Portugal Street and then along the entire length of Lincoln's Inn Fields. My leg was screaming with pain from the Jezail bullet wound it had taken not that many years ago, but I thought that a pajama-clad bare-footed man could hardly disappear into the crowd. If I could keep him in sight until I saw a constable or even an able-bodied athletic young man, I could shout for help. But at the corner of Newman's Row, he jumped into a small carriage, and it sped off.

Breathless and huffing and puffing like a steam engine, and with socks soaking wet from the morning grass, I returned to the hospital and climbed back up to the third floor. By the time I arrived, Holmes was standing and talking with Dr. Trevelyan and the supervising doctor. A constable stood with them. I assumed, correctly it turned out, that Holmes had deduced that the fellow in room 310 had only pretended to be catatonic and had been a plant of some anarchist organization intent on taking revenge on Count Myshkin. All the fellow had to do was distract the night nurse and the pour a vial of cyanide into the tea three places farther down the row of waiting cups.

"The only item," Holmes was saying, "that I have as yet no explanation for is why he waited around this morning instead of slipping away in the middle of the night."

The answer was given by a page boy who politely interrupted the conversation.

"Excuse me, gentlemen. But there are some men downstairs who say they have come to collect Count Myshkin. One of them says that his name is..." here the lad read from a card, slowly, "Prince Aleksei...Borisovich...Lobanov-Rostovskii. It says he is the Ambassador of the Russian Empire."

For a moment, we all just looked at each other and then Dr. Smythe-Harley quietly said, "Page, kindly return to the men from the Embassy and ask them to come to the third floor."

"What do we say to them?" I asked and then wished I had said nothing.

"Dr. Watson," said the hospital's senior doctor. "We tell them the unvarnished truth. No more, and no less."

A group of four men had appeared at the end of the hall and were following the page boy toward us. As they approached, one of them came forward and extended his hand to Holmes.

"Mr. Sherlock Holmes," he said. "Splendid to see you again. Our grateful thanks, sir. Words cannot express how indebted we are to you for the safe return of Count Myshkin. Please allow me to introduce our Ambassador. He himself is a member of the royal family. When I informed him of your contribution to the Czar's personal guard, he insisted on coming himself to meet you and taking the Count back to a home where he will be cared for until he recovers."

Holmes reticently extended his hand and shook that of the first secretary, and then he looked toward Dr. Smythe-Harley.

"Your Excellency," said the senior doctor, "I regret that we have very disturbing news that we must tell you."

He then explained in precise detail what had happened and led the way into Room 313 where the Russian visitors gathered around the now quite bluish body of the Count.

"Our hospital," said the doctor, "Takes full responsibility for this tragedy. It has taught us that we must endeavor to be far more thorough when admitting men to this floor and..."

"*Nyet*," interrupted the Ambassador. "It has taught to *us* that they are here...in London."

"*Who* are here?" asked Holmes.

"The *Narodnaya Volya*," said the Ambassador. "The anarchists. They have vowed to seize power from our Czar, and they are in league with similar minded men all over Europe. More are on their way. They will pretend to be Jews, who are coming here by the thousands. This one was waiting to kill me if he had a chance. Give this warning to your Scotland Yard. Good day gentlemen."

He turned and walked away quickly. The first secretary lingered behind and began to make arrangements for the removal of the body of the Count. I pulled my boots back on over my wet socks and Holmes and I returned to Baker Street. He was not in the mood to make conversation.

June passed into July, and then early August and a glorious summer settled on England. My medical practice was slowly growing and my prospects, so utterly absent when I returned to London from the Sub-Continent, were looking rather promising. Holmes had been hired by Inspectors Gregson and Lestrade of Scotland Yard and by two private clients to assist in several small cases. He had published his monograph on the use of plaster of Paris in the preservation of imprints from boots and shoes and had traveled overseas to assist, in a most confidential manner, the reigning family of Holland. He should have been pleased and satisfied with his success and growing reputation, but the moment a case had been completed, he returned to his armchair and opened yet anther book on the history of Russia or a magazine account of someone who had traveled there in the recent past.

I was nowhere near as diligent as Holmes in my reading, preferring to give cursory glances to the day's newspaper before picking up the *Sporting News* and silently cheering on my favorite teams. But I could not help but notice the stories, printed in the back pages of the newspapers, of the growing uprisings against the Jews. All across Eastern Europe, throughout the region known as the Pale of Settlement, where the Czars had permitted the Jews to live, the Christians had taken up arms against the Jewish communities and had smashed their windows, set fire to their homes, shops, and barns, beaten them and even killed some of them. The local police and soldiers were reported to have stood by idly and given no assistance to the victims.

These disturbances, which had been called *pogroms* by those concerned about them, had started not long after the assassination of the Czar. Some of the anarchists who were members of the *Narodnaya Volya* were Jewish and the powers that be had labeled the entire movement an act of the Hebrew people. The first persecution took place in Elizabethgrad in the Ukraine, but every day it seemed another one was reported. There did not appear to be any end in sight.

It id not take long for the turmoil to spread to England. I learned of it one afternoon in mid-August after completing my medical work for the day. As I was walking toward our door at 221B Baker Street, a police wagon pulled up to the pavement beside me. Out of it came the small and slightly stooped inspector that I had met during Holmes's investigation of the Jefferson Hope murders. The sloping forehead, beady eyes, and protruding mouth of Inspector Lestrade were unmistakable.

"Hello, Dr. Watson," he said as I held the door open for him. "Is Sherlock Holmes in?"

I replied saying that I was not sure but that I assumed he would be and both of us entered the front room. Holmes was sitting in his preferred armchair and reading a journal of some sort or other. He rose as we approached.

"Well, hello, Inspector. And to what do I owe the honor of your visit today? Please be seated. A bit too early for brandy, so some tea, perhaps?"

"I did not come here to pay a social call, Holmes," said Lestrade.

"It is a distinct possibility that I had already deduced that fact, Inspector," replied Holmes. "Pray then, how may I be of assistance to you?"

"You were involved in the murder of that Russian count in the hospital a few weeks back, right?"

"I was involved in identifying the murderer if that is what you mean."

"And in letting him get away, but that is beside the point. The point is that the entire mess has *not* gone away," said Lestrade.

"I would have thought," said Holmes, "that it had vanished given what appears to be the paucity of men and time you have assigned to it."

"For heaven' sake, Holmes. If a Russian comes to England and murders an Englishman, then *we* have a problem, and we are all over it. If a Russian comes to England and murders another Russian, then the Russians have a problem."

"Your sense of economy is understandable, Inspector," said Holmes. "What then has brought about the renewed interest?"

"Have you been reading the newspapers?" asked Lestrade.

"I assure you I have. To which story are you referring?"

"The good Christian people of Russia are giving the Jews of Russia more fresh hell every day."

"Ah, yes," said Holmes. "The pogroms have spread all over the Pale of Settlement. But how does that concern Scotland Yard?"

"Because the Jews are on the march. The greatest exodus since the Exodus had started. Our agents in Eastern Europe are telling us that as many as four million Jews may be leaving their homes and moving west. It has started already. Thousands have already departed from Kiev, Minsk, Warsaw, Odessa, Moscow, Kursk, Smolensk and a hundred other places I have never heard of. And at least half of them, maybe more, are coming here, to England."

"Good heavens," I exclaimed. "What in the world are we going to do with them?"

"We'll put as many as we can on boats and send them to America," said Lestrade. "But we expect that tens of thousands of them will stay here in England. That Jew, Disraeli, was all in favor of allowing them in. He's dead now, but Gladstone is of the same mind."

"Really, sir," I said. "I must object. The Earl of Beaconsfield converted to the Christian faith as a young man and died after receiving the sacraments."

"Did he now, Dr. Watson? Are you forgetting his campaign for equal rights for all the Jews in the Empire? And did he lose all his Jewish blood when he conveniently converted? I think not. And Gladstone is not much different. He opened Oxford and Cambridge to them and will not stop them from coming here. And you know what that means, do you not?"

"I assume," said Holmes, "that it means that the offerings of London's restaurants will greatly increase in quality and variety, but I fail to see the prospect of anything undesirable happening."

"What is means, Holmes, is that all those anarchists, who are recruiting all over the east of Europe as we speak, will pretend to be Jews even if they can't tell a bar mitzvah from a bar room, and they will move into Spitalfields. The core of them who are here now will help them find places to live and work, and before we know it, we are going to be overrun with anarchists."

"Some increase in their activity is possible," said Holmes, "although I fear your prediction is exaggerated. Surely, Scotland Yard and our customs officials demand to see some reasonable papers from would-be immigrants before allowing them to remain in Britain."

"Are you being deliberately obtuse, Holmes?" said Lestrade. "You know as well as I do that there are a dozen forgers-for-hire in the East End who will deliver a baptismal or birth certificate from a parish or synagogue in the Ukraine on an hour's notice. For a pound, you can have authentic papers dated back a hundred years. If an undesirable is determined to enter and stay in London, we are almost powerless to stop them. It is not as if we can build a great wall along our side of the Channel and keep them out."

"I admit," said Holmes, "such a wall would be silly. But what are you requesting me to do about it?"

"Holmes, you need to infiltrate the network of anarchists and find your murderer, the one you let get away. And you have to find all of his bomb tossing acquaintances. And you better get them into a prison before they can assist another thousand of the same ilk land and stay on English soil."

The inspector turned around and, without any parting words, departed.

"Do I recall," I said, "your saying something about not having any cases that were sufficiently demanding of your attention?" I could not resist a smile, perhaps a grin, directed at Holmes.

"It is possible that I might have uttered words to that effect," he said, rubbing his hands together and smiling back at me.

Chapter Four

The Irregulars Report

Over the next two weeks, I saw very little of Sherlock Holmes. By the time I reached the breakfast table in the morning, he had been and gone. When I retired to my bed in the evening, he had yet to re-appear. Occasionally I heard him enter and shuffle around the front room at some time after midnight. But on one Friday evening, nearly three weeks after Lestrade's visit, I happened to be sitting in my chair and reading a book, and in walked Holmes.

When he has set his mind on a case, his face seldom betrays any emotion other than steely determination, but on that evening, I could read the combination of frustration, disappointment, and weariness all over his countenance.

Without asking, I rose and walked to the sideboard and poured out a generous snifter of brandy and handed it to him. He looked up and offered a faint smile.

"Ah, my friend. Thank you."

"It would appear," I said, "that your efforts have not yet been successful."

"Not at all."

"Does Scotland Yard," I asked, "not have any informants who report on the immigrants in London?"

"Oh, yes," said Holmes. "Several. They referred me to three chaps who came from Russia in the past few years and who have quite acceptable English. I met with each of them."

"From the tone of your voice," I said, "I gather their services were not particularly useful."

"A complete waste of time. The first chap was a printer with a shop just off Brick Lane. Scotland Yard pays him a generous stipend to provide information and analysis. When I visited him, there were several customers in his shop, so I glanced at the books he had for sale. All were printed in Russian and in Cyrillic script. I assumed that he must be a person of some stature amongst the Russian immigrants who now live in London. As soon as his customers had departed, I introduced myself to him, and he immediately ushered me into the back of his shop leading me to believe that he indeed might have significant data to share with me. He wrote out a name and address on a card and handed it to me and then, *sotto voce*, said, 'You are never forget this name. This man should not on the streets of London be if to be safe.' I assumed that he had given me the name of the ringleader of the anarchists."

Holmes stopped momentarily to light a cigarette.

"And was he?" I asked.

"Ha! Not in the least. It was the printer's brother-in-law with whom he had been in a great spat for the past five years. He was a semi-literate fellow who I doubt could even spell *proletariat,* in any language, let alone leading a revolutionary cell. It was a complete waste of my time."

"And the others? Any better?"

"Worse. The second was the Orthodox priest at Saint Theophanes. The dear Papa Bezuhov told me to look in on some fellow named Tov Levin who, I was assured, not only was leading some of the anarchists here in London but was secretly involved in some horrible cult that was kidnapping and sacrificing children. It turned out that the fellow was the rabbi whose synagogue was around the corner, that both of them were religious enthusiasts for their own particular persuasion, and could not stand each other."

"And the third?"

"Ah, he took somewhat longer and wasted even more of my time. I must admit that he was exceptionally adept in discerning what it was I wanted to hear from him and then adjusting his information to meet my requests. For four days, he strung me along, but everything he told me was an utter fabrication. It was entirely a piece of fiction made up of whole cloth."

He expressed his obvious frustration by smacking down his cigarette into the ashtray and leaning back with a sigh.

"Was your brother of any help?" I asked.

"Mycroft? He put me in contact with several of the chaps in the Foreign Office who serve in our Embassies and Legations."

"You mean his spies?"

"Quite so, Watson, but he takes umbrage at my calling them that and quite frankly he has a point. They are utterly not worthy of the name *spies*. All they did, which was completely useless, was to write back and say 'Yes. There are rather a lot of Jews on the march, and it is possible that some anarchists might be among them, including those who are Catholic, Orthodox, and atheist.' Again, useless information, and a waste of my time."

"Have you any other way of penetrating the network?"

"I sent my beloved Irregulars out. They have proven to be highly reliable and persistent. They will report to me tomorrow morning at nine o'clock, and I expect that they will furnish some useful data. And now, as I am rather weary, I am going to bed. Goodnight, Watson."

At half-past eight the following morning, Holmes and I sat at the breakfast table. He had already checked his watch twice when I said, "Please, do relax. Have your Irregulars ever arrived early?"

He forced a smile and put away his watch. "You are right. It would be much more like them to be late. I will try to bide my time, but I admit that I am highly anxious to hear what they have to report. They are my last line of investigation at present."

He leaned back in his chair and forced himself to sip slowly on his tea. But then at ten minutes to nine, we heard the door on Baker Street open. Holmes looked at me and smiled.

"There is always a first time."

Then his smile vanished. The footsteps we heard ascending the seventeen steps were not those of a sprightly adolescent lad but of an adult male, and he was walking moving slowly. Into our room strode Inspector Lestrade.

"Good morning Holmes, Watson," he said as he walked toward the sofa and sat down. "Came to hear what you had learned. What have you got for me?"

"I regret that I have nothing to report as of yet."

"Scotland Yard is not paying you to come up empty, Holmes."

"And if I do not succeed in providing useful data, then my fee to Scotland Yard will be nothing," replied Holmes.

Lestrade folded his arms across his chest and harrumphed. "You know full well that we would rather pay you as generously as possible and that you help us accordingly."

Holmes nodded. "I appreciate your offer. I will be receiving another report within the hour, and I expect that it will have some degree of utility. Might I ask if you have learned anything that might be of assistance to me?"

"Just one item, and it has meant that I have had to pull my men from gathering intelligence and assign them to patrol Kensington."

"Good heavens," I said. "Why in the world would you have to do that?"

"Because the Duke of Edinburgh landed his ship in Portsmouth yesterday and he is coming into London for the next week."

"But why? What has he to do with anything? Who would want to harm him?" I asked, utterly in the dark.

Prince Albert, the Duke of Edinburgh and second son of Queen Victoria, was well-known to the English populace. He had entered the Royal Navy at the age of fourteen and had risen, in his own right — or as much as a royal can accomplish anything in his own right — to the post of admiral and would soon be assuming command of the Channel Fleet out of the naval base in Portsmouth. Most of his life was spent at sea, but when he returned to London he was generally quite popular with the common people.

"Nobody wants to harm him," said Lestrade, "except perhaps for the music lovers of London."

"Music lovers?" I asked.

"He fancies himself a violinist, but his sound is even more wretched than that of Sherlock Holmes. By rights, he should be shot before he has a chance to inflict his screeching on the ears of humanity."

Lestrade gave a smug smile, and Holmes responded with a forced "Ha. Ha."

"But," continued Lestrade, "it is not the Duke, it's the Duchess we're worried about. When the Duke's away, she seldom ventures out beyond the gates of Kensington Palace, but he likes to go trotting through the parks and enjoying the friendly adulation of the crowds. She will have to ride along beside him."

While the Duke was quite popular with the people, his wife, the Duchess of Edinburgh was not. They thought her snobbish and snooty and, in turn, she responded with contempt and disdain.

"Merciful heavens," I said. "Why her? Nobody likes her, but that is hardly a reason to attack her."

Lestrade replied, "Have you forgotten who she was before marrying Prince Alfred?"

I had.

"Her name," said Holmes, "was Grand Duchess Maria Alexandrovna, the only surviving daughter of Czar Alexander II, the recently assassinated although selectively mourned Emperor of Russia."

"That is exactly who she is," said Lestrade. "And she will be a sitting duck for anyone who has it in for the house of Holstein-Gottorp-Romanov."

"Were you tipped off by one of your informants?" asked Holmes.

"Those charlatans? They are worse than useless. No, one of my men, Athelney Jones, noted the announcement in the press and made the reasonable conclusions that she could be a target."

"Ah, yes, Jones," said Holmes. "He can be as fierce as a tiger physically, but I would not have expected such a flash of imagination. Please give him my regards."

"If you think that would matter to him, I will," said Lestrade. "Now, I have to be on my way. But if your report this morning reveals anything worthwhile, I expect to be informed forthwith."

He departed, and Holmes returned to his now cold tea. He checked his watch again, this time to confirm that the captain of the Baker Street Irregulars was late as usual.

At half past nine, a knock came to the door, and I smiled at Holmes. I had expected to hear the steps of a young man bounding up the stairs, but the steps I heard were moving slowly and even stopped part way up, before continuing.

Gordon Wiggins, the handsome, lithe, and usually in need of a bath, captain of the Irregulars entered the room. He was not beaming a grin as he normally did when he came to report.

"I 'ave come ta report, Mr. Holmes, sir," he said.

"Excellent, Captain Wiggins," said Holmes. "please deliver your report."

"Am terrible sorry, Mr. Holmes. But there is really nothin' to report, sir. We've bin trying' sir, we've bin tryin' we 'ave. Honest we 'ave, sir. You tol' us to lolly 'round Spitalfields and get to know some of the Rooshin boys, an' recruit them to be Irregulars, sir, an' we tried, honest, we did, sir. But they were just off the boat, sir. An' none of them speaks English. An' they is all serious, sir, an' they spen' all their spare time helpin' in their pa's shops an' such, an' when they is not doin' that, they is goin' to the school to learn English, sir. So we tried, but we couldna get through to them no how. Terrible sorry, sir. We're all prepared we are to give you back your shillin's seein' as we failed, sir."

Holmes's entire body appeared to droop with disappointment, but he managed a warm smile at Wiggins.

"No Wiggins, tell my boys to keep their shillings. I dare say I should have known that such an assignment might be impossible."

"Well sir, we are hopin' that you won't be forgettin' about us and that you will still want to use us Irregulars, sir. We all like to be workin' for Mr. Sherlock Holmes, sir."

"I would never forget you, my dear lad," said Holmes. "In fact, I have a new assignment for all of you. And don't be thinking that it is not important just because it will be far easier than the last one."

"Really sir? A new one? For all of us?"

"As many soldiers as you can muster, Wiggins. How many are there of you now?" asked Holmes.

"Hard to say, Mr. Holmes, sir. What with the boys comin' and goin' and their families doin' the same. But I think if we called them all in, we might find nigh on to thirty of us for you, sir."

"Excellent. We need every one of you. I assume you know where Kensington Palace is."

The young fellow's eyes went wide.

"Sure ... we know where 'tis, sir. But we never get ta go near there, sir. That place an' the parks are for the posh folks, sir, not the like o' us."

"Well then, you will have to pretend to be posh. I am going to need every one of you, and I will pay every boy a shilling a day."

"A shillin' a day? For each o' us?"

Wiggins gave a low whistle.

"Blimey, it must be important. Are we guardin' the ol' girl herself? The Queen?"

"Ah, very close, Wiggins. Not the Queen but her son, the Duke of Edinburgh, and his wife, the Duchess. Over the next few days, starting Monday, the day after tomorrow, they will be riding out of the palace gates and trotting slowly through Kensington Gardens and Hyde Park and greeting the common people. Now, there is a good chance that a few of the people will not be decent English folk but ... what did you call them? ...Rooshins? Yes, some might be from Russia. You know the type, Wiggins. Dark hair that needs to be cut, dark eyebrows, workman's cap, scruffy beard."

"Oh, we know them blokes, right, we do sir. We can spot 'em a mile away."

"Brilliant, Wiggins. When you do spot them on Monday, you must follow them all the way back to Spitalfields and then come and report to me as to what shop or what lodgings they entered. Is that understood, Wiggins?"

"Oh, yes, Mr. Holmes. The lads'll be right chuffed ta hear, sir. An' thank you, sir, for still trustin' us after lettin' you down an' all."

The young man's face was beaming, and he turned and descended the stairs, some three at a time and slammed the door with such energy that I expected Mrs. Hudson to be after him with her rolling pin.

After he had departed, I turned to Holmes.

"Not worried that you are cutting it a bit too fine? What if these anarchist chaps try to take a shot at the Duchess tomorrow?"

"They are creatures of habit, Watson. They must have observed the Czar for days, if not weeks, before knowing the exact time and place to roll the bomb under his carriage. No, these dissident types are impatient for revolutionary change, but they have learned to be patient when planning their attacks. They have all this week until the Duke's shore leave is over. I warrant they have planned to watch for three days if not four before striking. If my lads can do their jobs, and I have full faith in them, we should be able to round the whole rum lot of them up before they have a chance to try anything."

"Very well, Holmes. I hope you are right."

He merely smiled at me and strode over to his chemistry table. It was still just mid-morning, so I decided to take myself for a long walk, one that would take me to Kensington Palace, through the gardens and the park and back again.

The weekend newspapers all had the story of the visit of Prince Alfred, the Duke of Edinburgh. Each paper attempted to outdo its rivals by revealing more details of the plans of the Duke and Duchess. The exact times of their public appearances were given as was the route of their planned rides. Maps were included showing precisely where well-wishers could stand to wave and, if they were fortunate, shake the Duke's hand as he passed. He was quite the popular member of the royal family. Unlike his older brother, the Prince of Wales, or 'Bertie' as he was called, the Duke was a thorough-going responsible man, and already an admiral of the fleet. A shame, said many of the wags, that Bertie could not be sent away to play with his mistresses and the Duke allowed to ascend to the throne when the old girl passed on to her eternal reward.

I found myself somewhat in agreement with that idea, even if there was no chance of its ever happening. I had strolled over to Kensington and tried to think about where I would stand if I wanted to shoot at a member of the Royal Family and imagined tipping my hat to the Duke and the Duchess as they passed by. The Duchess was not at all popular with the common people, but it was generally acknowledged that she was an attractive woman, or at least as attractive as the English would ever consider a Russian to be.

I would have much preferred not to have to attend to the needs of my patients on Monday and to have gone to Kensington myself, but again, that was not to be. So, I put in my solid eight hours of poking and prodding the diminishing bodies of over two dozen English souls to whom time and gravity were not friends.

.

Chapter Five

No Dead Russian on Her Majesty's Lawn

I closed the door of my office at the end of the day and prepared to take a leisurely walk back to Baker Street. I took a newspaper from the first newsboy I encountered, and suddenly I was no longer walking slowly. I was running and reading at the same time. The headline read:

ATTEMPTED ASSINATION OF PRINCE ALFRED
SHOT FIRED AT DUKE OF EDINBURGH.
SAVED BY HEROIC SCHOOLBOYS.

The rest of the story ran as follows:

A near tragedy was narrowly avoided this morning in Kensington Gardens. Prince Alfred, the Duke of Edinburgh and his wife, the Duchess, were enjoying their ride and were greeting the English people when a man ran out from the crowd, stood behind the Duchess and raised a revolver. A schoolboy, who remains unidentified, reacted bravely and flung a stone at the would-be cowardly assassin, striking him. The shot went off, but it was far wide of the mark of the back of the Duke. The same boy quickly stepped out from the crowd and hurled sharp stones at the haunches of the horses, causing them to bolt and gallop away, removing the Duke and the Duchess from further danger. The life of the Duke was spared.

The man with the revolver turned and ran pell-mell in the direction of Bayswater and several brave boys tore after him. They were joined by at least a score of other lads who seemed determined to pounce on their prey. Behind them, a dozen fleet-footed bobbies were in hot pursuit. The killer at one point turned and shot his revolver directly toward the boys, but they kept on closing in on him. As luck would have it, there was a carriage waiting for him at the street, and he leapt in and sped away just inches from the grasping hands of the pack of courageous young men.

Witnesses were of one mind is saying that the assassin was obviously not English. "He was dark and swarthy," said one lady. "His clothes needed washed and pressing. Not an Englishman at all." "And he was a coward," said Mr. Ewan Barnstopple of Sussex Gardens. "Only a cowardly foreigner would hide behind a woman's skirts. He snuck in behind the Duchess and was going to use her as a shield to protect himself as he fired on the Duke. That's something that a Frenchman or an Italian would do, but never an Englishman."

This newspaper asked Scotland Yard how it had been possible that an assassin could have come so close to killing a much-loved member of the royal family. Inspector Lestrade replied by saying, "Constables were in place all along the route and were already in action as soon as the man emerged from the crowd, but no one expects a full-grown policeman to be as fast and agile as a plucky English schoolboy. Those lads were the heroes of the days, and we must give them all possible credit. We must remember that it was brave English schoolboys who won the Battle of Waterloo and if they will present themselves at Scotland Yard, citations for their bravery will be awarded. Meanwhile, we will be rounding up all the usual suspects and not letting up until the cowardly madman and his accomplices, if he had any, have been brought to justice."

Anyone knowing who these brave lads were is asked to convey that information to Scotland Yard so that well-earned rewards may be granted.

It was only a few years ago, in Sydney that another anarchist tried to kill Prince Alfred. Unfortunately, there were no plucky English schoolboys there on that occasion, and the Duke was wounded. He recovered and has gone on to an esteemed career in the Fleet.

"These boys," said the Duke of Edinburgh after the commotion had died down, "would make fine sailors in the British Fleet. I would be proud to have them as members of my ship any day."

And so would we all.

By the time I had read and re-read the story, I was climbing the stairs to our rooms on Baker Street. Our dear Mrs. Hudson greeted me at the second floor and thrust a glass of iced lemon into my hand.

"Having you faint from the heat won't help the Prince," she said. "Now just stop and catch your breath and wipe the sweat off your forehead and then you can join the rest of them."

The rest of them, gathered in our front room, were Sherlock Holmes, Inspector Lestrade, Assistant Inspector Athelney Jones, three other chaps that I did not recognize but who had a senior government grey look to them and, in the corner, was an older, heavier fellow whose features gave him away. He was, I deduced correctly, Mycroft Holmes. For him to leave the *sanctum sanctorum* of his office in Whitehall and come to his younger brother's rooms on Baker Street was a highly unusual occurrence.

One of the civil servants glared at me as I entered the room.

"Stop," he said as I entered the room. "I do not know who you are, but you are forbidden to enter this room. This is a confidential meeting of Her Majesty's government and only open to those who have permission. Leave now."

Before I could sputter my indignant response, Sherlock Holmes intervened.

"Ah, Doctor Watson. Welcome. Please come in and take a seat if you wish. Gentlemen, Dr. Watson is the lessee of these rooms so it is he who must give permission to you to hold a meeting. So, Dr. Watson, may we please hold a meeting in your premises?"

He gave me a slight wink as he spoke and I played along.

"Oh, very well. If you must, and Her Majesty has nowhere else to have a meeting, then I suppose you can have a meeting here. Please, gentlemen, as you were. Pray continue."

I ignored the hostile glares and walked across the room and sat down in the empty chair beside Mycroft Holmes.

"Keep going," growled Mycroft Holmes to government men. "just ignore Dr. Watson."

The senior bureaucrat resumed his interrogation of Lestrade and Holmes.

"Very well, then. Let us get this straight. There were a score of bobbies along the route and then a host of street urchins. Now, Mr. Holmes, what did you call these boys?"

"The Baker Street Irregulars."

"And why in the world do you call them that?"

"Primarily because they live in the vicinity of Baker Street and are irregular," replied Holmes.

"Right, and so is my Aunt Belinda quite irregular. But how is it that they were all over Kensington Gardens this morning?"

"I had suspected that an attack might take place this week and I had sent them there to see if they might identify a likely killer and follow him home."

"Right, which they failed to do. But they appear to be excellent in the skill of throwing stones."

"I rather liken them," said Holmes, "to Davids up against Goliath."

"A bit of an exaggeration given that Goliath ended up dead and your quarry escaped in a carriage. But nevertheless, we are grateful for what they were able to accomplish, which is more that we can say for Scotland Yard."

"My men," said Lestrade, "performed exactly as they were could be expected to do."

"If by that," said the interrogator, "you mean they were expected to have the Duchess shot, then I assume you are correct. And I do understand, do I not, that you are both telling me that it was the Duchess who was their target, not the Duke."

Both Holmes and Lestrade nodded their affirmation.

"And do you expect that they will try another time?"

Holmes and Lestrade again confirmed their expectation.

"Well then, all that Her Majesty can demand of both of you is that you infiltrate this organization and do it quickly. The Foreign Office and the Cabinet do not want Russian royalty getting murdered in London. Is that understood? And don't ask me how you plan to do it, and if it is better that we not know, so be it. Just do it. Is that understood?"

Lestrade and Holmes both nodded obediently. The three chaps from Her Majesty departed, leaving Mycroft Holmes behind.

"Sherlock and Lestrade," he said. "I do not give a tinker's damn how you do it, but you bloody well better find out who is killing Russian counts and trying to kill Russian princesses and stop them. Great Britain needs to be on friendly terms with Russia now that our squabbles in Central Asia have subsided. So, between the two of you, make this nonsense stop, before anyone else is killed."

He then likewise departed, descended the stairs, entered his polished carriage, and rumbled south on Baker Street.

"Holmes," said Lestrade, "we have to follow the rules of the book. You do not. Under normal circumstances, that would gall me no end. Today, I withdraw my objections. Do whatever it takes. One dead Russian and almost two is all I ever want to have to deal with. And I assure you that Her Majesty herself does not want a dead son or daughter-in-law on her front lawn."

He then took his leave. Holmes and I just looked at each other, both giving shrugs of apparent hopelessness. Then he walked over to the window and gave a wave of his hand.

"We will see what my boys have to report. They must be down on the pavement and waiting for our guests to leave."

An immediate knock sounded from the door and moments later Gordon Wiggins entered the room. I had expected that he would be thoroughly pleased with himself and his Irregulars, what with being hailed as heroes in the Press, but he looked rather crestfallen as he shuffled into the room.

"Congratulations," said Holmes, "on saving the life of the Prince and Duchess. All of England is talking about you."

"Right, Mr. Holmes, sir. I suppose they are, sir."

"You must be very proud of your lads. You have become famous."

"Yes, sir, Mr. Holmes sir. I guess it's a bit of all right."

"Then why the long face, Captain Wiggins?"

"Sorry, sir, You're right. We should be chuffed, sir. We'll try to be more like that, sir," he said and forced a smile. "But, well, you see, Mr. Holmes, sir, it's just that you had told us that you might need us for four or five days and maybe a week. So, we were all lookin' forward to getting' a shillin' a day for all that time and just to lolly 'round Kensington Gardens and watch all the toffs and the common folk and it were the most pleasant task you ever give us, sir. But now it's come and gone after just one day, sir. So, we're happy to have done what we could but are sore missin' what we thought was bang up the elephant for a whole week, sir."

Holmes smiled warmly at the lad. "Ah, yes, of course. How thoughtless of me not to make the terms of your contracts more explicit. I had agreed to pay a shilling a day for up to a week and I shall honor my agreement. That is what is required by British Common Law, Wiggins. So, you may tell your lads that they shall have their full pay."

The young fellow's eyes lit up like street lights. "You mean, sir, we will have seven shillin's a piece, sir? Even if we do not have to work for you, sir?"

"Six," said Holmes. "As an enlightened employer, I do not send young men off to work on Sundays."

"Ooow, that's jolly good, sir. Can I go now and tell the boys? They'll be over the moon."

"No, Wiggins, not yet. I must have an account of what took place this morning in Kensington. You must deliver a full and complete report as part of your contractual agreement, young man. Now, stand and deliver."

The boy was grinning from ear to ear and was having to make a severe effort to concentrate, but he took a breath and began to state his report.

"Well, sir, like you told us, sir, we lined up all along the route the Prince and the Duchess were going to be ridin'. I put one of my boys every fifty yards and I told them that as soon as the Prince had passed them they had to run ahead o' the rest and get back inta the line further along. A bit like playin' leap frog, if you know what I mean, sir."

"An excellent strategy, Wiggins," said Holmes. "Continue."

"On the first leg, what started at the Palace, there was nothin' took place and we just kept runnin' to keep up and it were getting' harder on account o' the crowds were getting' more and more and we had to push ourselves ta the front of the line. But we kept doin' that."

"Excellent work. Quite brilliant," said Holmes.

"I have to confess, sir. There was a bit of luck as well, sir."

"Indeed, and how was that?"

"Well, sir. We have this one Irregular and we call him Prince Bertie, sir. He's a bit of an odd one, he is, sir, but he was the true hero of the day."

"I have not met this boy. Tell me abut him."

"Very good, sir. He's about my own age but one of the queerest lookin' boys you ever see. He's got a bit of a snub nose and flat brow and common face, he does, sir. And he's as dirty an Irregular as you would ever wish to see, sir. But he has all the airs and manners of a gentleman, sir."

"Ah, does he now? And is that why you call him Prince Bertie?"

"That and a bit more sir. You see he's a bit short for his age and has rather bow legs, and, well, he's a right chubby chap he is, just like the Prince of Wales, so that's more the reason."

"And how was it that this chubby little fellow became the hero. From what you have said, I doubt he could run fast enough to keep up with anyone."

"Oh, he can run fast sir, just not for very far. And he is no good at all at sports, and cannot fight worth a farthin'. So, he's taught himself how to look after himself. He practiced and practiced, he did, at throwin' rocks and stones. He became so good that he can hit a rabbit on the run. So, if someone is lookin' to do him no good he takes a stone out his pocket and lets it fly. He wears a man's coat which reaches down to his heels and has several large pockets. And he always keeps a supply of rocks that are the perfect size for pitchin' at someone."

"So, he was the one who hit the killer and the horses."

"Yes, sir. That was him, sir. The rest of us give chase after the fellow. But it was Prince Bertie what saved the Prince and Duchess. He was him, sir."

"Excellent, well then, you must give him one extra shilling and thank him for his diligence. And make sure you hold on to him. It seems you have quite the brilliant recruit there, Wiggins. Well done."

"We do our best for you, Mr. Holmes, sir."

Holmes clapped the young man on his shoulder and sent him on his way but then he sat down slowly in his chair and again fell into silence.

"Twice, Watson, twice. We have nearly had him and he has escaped. How now do we go after him?"

I was quite certain that he was not actually requesting a response from me, but I offered a thought all the same.

"Well then, Holmes," I said. "If we can no longer go to them are we at the place where Mohammed and the mountain must ..." but then I stopped. I could never get that couplet straight as to who and what was to go to the other, and we were dealing with men pretending to be Jews, not Mohammedans.

Holmes gave me a bit of a condescending sidewards look. Then, quite abruptly, his look changed to one where he was lost in thought. Slowly, a glimmer of a smile appeared.

"Watson, your feeble and failing attempt at wit may have inadvertently contained a trace of brilliance. It just may be possible that we will have to make the mountain come to us."

I was in a fog on that one. "Whatever are you saying?" I demanded.

"Tomorrow is Saturday, and you do not have any patients, do you? Excellent. Please be ready to come with me by eight o'clock. We will find breakfast at our destination."

"Will I need my service revolver?" I asked.

"I should think not. But both of us will have to don disguises."

He turned immediately and began to rifle through his recently assembled pile of books, journals, and newspapers that all contained content related to Russia. When I began to ask him something, he raised his hand to silence me. We ate supper in silence, and I passed the evening reading the latest Bulwer-Lytton novel.

Chapter Six

Our Enterprise in Spitalfields

"Spitalfields Market," Holmes said to the cab driver when the next morning had arrived. "The entrance on Lamb Street, please."

"Right, sir," replied the driver. "off to do your shoppin' are ye?"

"To purchase some of the delicious delicacies," said Holmes.

Holmes had supplied me with a wig of rather messy black hair, an untidy black mustache, and a set of eyeglasses made of clear glass with heavy dark rims. He had placed one of his favorite wigs on his head, the one with long white hair that he used when he pretended to be a clergyman or an aging bookseller. I thought we looked ridiculous but agreed that had we been dressed as gentlemen we would have stood out like sore thumbs in the market.

As there was very little traffic on a Saturday morning, we were at the market in good time, but already the crowds had invaded the stalls, looking for bargains in fresh fruit and vegetables, new or used clothing, dry goods, household items, and just about everything imaginable that could be used by a working class or immigrant family. It was also a well-known fact that if anything were ever stolen from your home, you could buy it back at Spitalfields at about a third of the price you originally paid for it on the high street.

"Are we to wade into the masses of the great unwashed?" I asked Holmes as we stood on the pavement on Lamb Street.

"Oh, no. There is no need for us to enter. We are going to walk around the boundary."

"Jolly good, then. What are we looking for?"

"A spacious place to eat."

"Spacious? Is that the only criterion?" I asked. "Might not we also look for one that served decent food?"

"Oh, no. That will not be necessary. We are going to buy or lease the establishment and change the menu."

"Are we, now? And what do you know about operating a pub or restaurant, Holmes?"

"This morning, nothing at all. But the Countess does."

"Who?" I asked.

"The Countess. You must remember her. The Russian woman from Wisconsin who had her amber tiara stolen last year."

"You mean Betsy Burdukovsky? The pump American lady that told everyone she was a distant cousin of the Czar? That countess?"

"The very one, Watson."

"Holmes, she's a long way down queer street, if I remember correctly."

"There is nothing wrong with your memory, except you may have forgotten that she speaks native Russian and appears to know almost every member of the Russian ghetto in London. And, I suspect, she is, as always, in need of more money. She is meeting us here any moment, although she will most likely be late, and together we are going to find an appropriate establishment and turn it into the most popular of all the Russian pubs and salons in London."

"There are no Russian pubs or salons in London," I said.

"Then it shall not be difficult to be the most popular," replied Holmes.

It was a quarter of an hour before nine o'clock when a carriage stopped at the curb and out of it climbed a woman of a certain age and a certain magnitude, holding a small dog. Both she and the poor cur were wrapped in sable stoles even though it was now August. For a fleeting moment, I thought that a call to the Royal Humane Society might be in order.

She cruised along the pavement toward us, and the dog did not seem to be overly distressed. As we were disguised, neither she nor the dog recognized Holmes. He accosted her with an exaggerated bow and in a whisper revealed his identity.

"Oooh ... my ... goodness. Sheeerlock! daaaawlink, how wonderful to see you. Look at you. You should have stayed on stage, dawlink. I have missed you terribly. You never come to my salon for caviar and vodka anymore. Why just yesterday I was telling Viscount Devonport all about the magnificent time you retrieved my amber tiara. Goodness knows, it would have cost me five thousand pounds to replace it, I told him. But Sherlock Holmes returned it to me and, being such a perfect gentleman, refused to accept even a modest reward. Such a perfect gentleman you are Sherlock, daaawlink."

She held out her hand and Holmes graciously took it and bowed to kiss it.

"To what do I owe the honor," she said, "of having Sherlock Holmes request my presence at such an ungodly hour in Spitalfields Market, of all the God-forsaken places?"

"It is a business proposition, my dear Countess," said Holmes. "One in which there is the prospect of *mnogo deneg* for you if it all comes to fruition."

"Oh, *Bozha moy*," the Countess said. "Very well, pray tell."

Holmes told her, as he had me, of his plan to open a Russian pub and salon in the Spitalfields neighborhood.

"And you, my dear Countess, shall be the consulting expert helping me choose the staff, the furnishings, and the menu. It must be authentically Russian even if you are not."

"Daaarlink, how glorious. I shall have caviar sent in from Odessa, and *Isteeney* vodka from St. Petersburg. Oh ... you must excuse me for a moment. My dear friend, Anastasiya, the cousin of my charwoman, has a stall just up ahead on the right. She makes the most utterly divine Marie biscuits, and I must have one. Oh dear ... I appear to have left my purse in my house. Sherlock, be a darling and slip a five-pound note into my hand. Oh, you are such a dear. Now don't run away whilst I am gone."

She walked over to a stall selling baked goods and chatted on loudly with the proprietress, accompanied by gales of laughter. We waited for ten minutes until she returned, whereupon Holmes introduced her to me. She held out her hand for me to bow and kiss. I was half tempted to grab it firmly and pump it in a manly handshake, but fearing that I might send the poor dog toppling onto the pavement, I acquiesced and graciously kissed her sausage-like fingers.

"I am afraid, my dear," said Holmes, "that the level of cuisine will be closer to peasant class than nobility. We will be catering to the great *lumpenproletariat*."

The dear lady's face took on a look of being utterly aghast.

"*Nevozmozhnah*. That is not possible. I would not know where to begin. If I am to help you, it must be a select establishment. I could not dream of anything less."

Holmes smiled, leaned in closely to the buxom dowager, and whispered.

"Countess, it is a clandestine assignment requested directly by the house of the Czar. The funds are being advanced by the Foreign Office, and the project is being undertaken because of the attempt recently on the life of the Duchess of Edinburgh. I assume you read about it in the press."

The lady's eyes went very wide and her mouth dropped open, causing yet another chin to appear.

"Why, of course, I read about it. But the reports said that some madman was trying to kill the Duke, not my dear Maria. Who would want to hurt her? She is such a dear, and so beloved of the English people."

"But not," said Holmes, "of some of the anarchists in Russia. Now, do not ask me to disclose anything else. I have been bound to secrecy by the Office of the Cabinet."

A look of awe and incredulity came over the dowager's face, and she puffed out her already puffed-out bosom.

"Very well," she said. "If it is for Czar and country, then we will just have to do what is required of us. Mother Russia expects every woman to do her duty. Where shall we start?"

"We search for the spacious venue that is required for our future customers."

We continued to walk around the exterior boundaries of the market, stopping in at several small pubs and shops before declaring them unsuitable. At the corner of Fournier and Commercial Streets, we stopped and looked at the corner pub, *The Ten Bells*. It was a longstanding establishment in Spitalfields, even longer than the lovely commissioned edifice, Christ Church Spitalfields, that had been erected across the road and whose admonishing presence had done nothing to discourage the reprobate habits of the loyal customers of the pub.

Before ten o'clock in the morning, any pub in London is not likely to be offering much in the way of ale or other spirits, but this large operation was advertising a full English breakfast, so we entered and assumed the role of famished shoppers.

A pretty young redhead pranced up to our table and gave us a friendly if saucy smile. Her dress was cut somewhat lower in the front than was fashionable, but that must be what was needed to help the male customers wake up and become a bit more cheerful first thing in the morning.

"Good morning, lady and gentlemen," she said. "My name is Mary Kelly, and how may I be of service to the three of you this fine morning?"

We ordered our breakfasts, but then Holmes made an additional request.

"Miss Kelly, as you do not appear to be particularly busy at this hour, might we request a few minutes of your time and ask some questions about this fine establishment where you work? I would be happy to compensate you appropriately for your service. And put in an order for yourself as well."

The young thing smiled and said, "Right. Why, of course, always happy to fulfill our customers' requests. Give me a minute to pass your order into the kitchen, and I will return straightaway."

Holmes thanked her, and she gave a friendly smile to all three of us. I returned it.

"Always does my heart good," I said, "to see a young English lass who is not afraid of hard work and makes a valiant effort to be cheerful in the morning. This must be just the start of her shift for the day, and a long day ahead. A fine, hard-working young lass, I must say."

Holmes and the Countess exchanged glances and simultaneously rolled their eyes.

"What?" I said. "Are you two so backward that you do not approve of a young woman having an income of her own?"

The Countess broke out laughing.

"Oh, my dear doctor," she said. "It is wonderful, absolutely wonderful, that there are in this world a few gentlemen like you still alive. But, daaarlink, I hate to inform you that the sweet young thing is at the end of her shift, not the beginning. And she most certainly has an income of her own, earned while horizontal, in addition to whatever she is paid to serve breakfast."

I was mortified. "Why, are you saying that this young lady is a woman of ill repute? Why, in the name of all that is holy, would you come to such a vile conclusion."

Holmes sighed. "My dear doctor, just looking at her cheerful face you can detect dark circles under her eyes, indicating that she is need of several hours' sleep. There are traces of bruising on her chest that even the application of powder cannot fully hide. And her gait is somewhat bow-legged. These are obvious indications of her primary profession."

I was quite distressed by what he said and began immediately to try to think of some means of rescuing this girl and others like her from the clutches of depravity. When she returned, all smiles, to our table, I found it difficult to look at her without blushing.

She set out our plates, laden with a complete complement of delicious, steaming English breakfast foods.

"Miss Mary," began Holmes, "permit me to identify ourselves. This fine lady is Countess Burdukovsky, an esteemed member of the Russian society who now chooses to call London home. Because of some of the recent troubles in Russia, she is seeking opportunities to invest her assets in profitable enterprises here in London. One of the potential targets for her investments might be this pub."

"Garn," said Miss Mary. "You must be mad. This place? Just look around. It's nigh on to empty. It had some good years far in the past, but the neighborhood has been changin', and the customers are vanishing."

"And why is that, Miss?"

"Well, sir, there has been a public house on this site for at least a hundred years. At least that's what Annie Chapman tells me. She's been workin' here for much longer than I have, so she knows a lot more than I do. Years and years ago, it was a goin' concern, it was. But then all those Frenchies moved in. They called them the Huge Nots on account of all the things they would not do. They would not drink, and not use tobacco, and not dance, and not go to a music hall, and not do any of those things that we like to think of as making life passably worth living and all they did was work at their weaving all day and gather in their basements in the evening for prayers and Bible reading. Well, they all prospered and moved out, and so we had a few good years of fine English and some Irish folks living in Spitalfields, but this past year we have been flooded with hundreds of Russians. Thousands, maybe. But they're almost all Jews and no more given to having a glass of ale or a wee dram of whiskey than the Frenchmen were. When Miss

Annie started working here a decade ago, she says that she made a decent living off her wages and the little extras what the customers gave her. But now, it's a hard go for all of us. If you're thinking of making an investment in Spitalfields, I would not be recommending this place. No sir. And no ma'am."

"Miss, you have been most helpful," said Holmes as he slid a sovereign over to her. "we wish you a very fine day and cannot thank you enough. Before you go, might you be so kind as to tell us the name of the publican who owns this fine establishment?"

"Why thank you, sir. The gent, if you want to call him that, who is the proprietor of The Ten Bells goes by the name of Shamus Maguire. He's in the back office this morning toting up the receipts from last night if you want to meet him. He's a pleasant enough man and fair and decent to the likes of Annie and me, as long as we do our part to keep the customers satisfied, that is."

"Ah, why thank you, again, miss," said Holmes. "If we speak with him we shall be sure to let him know that you have done a brilliant job looking after us."

The young lady — and I still wished to think of her in that way — rose and departed. We finished eating our breakfast, and I assumed that we would now move on in an effort to find whatever it was that Holmes was looking for.

"I would hope," I said, "that somewhere not too far away is an establishment more to your liking than this place."

"On the contrary," said Holmes. "This pub would appear to be ideal for our needs."

I was surprised and perplexed by the illogic of what he said.

"Come now, Holmes," I said. "You heard what the barmaid said. This place is struggling as a business. If you took it over you would be sure to lose a small fortune. It is far too large for its present clientele. The overhead would be ruinous. How can you possibly say that it would be good for you?"

"For precisely those reasons. Now, let us find our way into the back offices and try to speak to the Irish publican. I suspect that he would be eager to entertain an offer."

Mr. Shamus Maguire was indeed interested in the offer made by Sherlock Holmes. To his credit, Mr. Maguire exhibited a paternal concern for his employees and would not hear of their being dismissed with no compensation. I had no doubt that he also wanted to make sure that they would all be ready to return to work as soon as required once our lease expired.

By the time our meeting had finished, the Countess and Holmes had full rights to take over the premises beginning the following fortnight but would have to pay the lordly sum of £1,000 to cover the six-month lease and the wages of the Ten Bells' employees.

"Merciful heavens, Holmes," I said after we had departed the office. "Where are you going to get £1,000? You have hardly enough at the end of each month to pay our rent."

"I am quite certain, my dear friend," he replied, "that with a modicum of mental exertion you can answer that question for yourself."

The image of Mycroft Holmes appeared immediately in my mind. I asked no further questions.

Chapter Seven

Counting Up Dead Counts

During the next two weeks, as I returned to our rooms on Baker Street each day after attending to my medical practice, I was met by the sight of Holmes and the Countess huddled over sets of plans and documents.

The Countess, I finally discovered, was the only daughter of Russian peasants who had emigrated some forty years earlier to America and had prospered as dairy farmers on a large tract of land just west of Oshkosh. Miss Betsy, as she was known before awarding herself the title of countess, departed from her life of attending to cows and vats of cheese the day she turned eighteen. She made her way to Europe and took on her new identity with a passion. Regrettably, she had acquired an irresistible taste for rich dairy products, and they had taken their toll on her physique, but that did not in any way slow her down. She appeared to be having a delightful time planning the newest pub and restaurant in London.

"We are going to call it *The Balalaika,*" she told me. "Now, I ask you, my dear doctor, isn't that just a perfect name?"

I nodded my agreement and later searched my reference books to find out what in the world a *balalaika* was.

"I was horrified," she said, "that Mr. Holmes here would not allow me to feature caviar on the menu, but we shall have the most delectable borscht and zakuski for the first course, with a choice beef stroganoff, golubtsy, knishes, salyanka, and unlimited bliny and potatoes for the main course, all served with mounds of black bread. On every table, there will be a constant supply of *stoli*. I assure you that every poor Russian peasant who is homesick for the Motherland will become our patron. I have found a glorious group of *babushkas* who are thrilled to be able to cook their traditional foods in great quantities, and a dozen beautiful young women, every one of them a perfect *krasavitsa*, to serve the tables. They will all answer to the name *Natasha*. Flyers announcing the event will be posted all over Spitalfields. We shall be completely overwhelmed with customers. It will be utterly faaaabulous. And very profitable."

"But ...," I said. "You are going to end up with anybody and everybody coming. How will you ever spot an anarchist amongst them?"

"That, my dear doctor," she said, "I will leave to Mr. Sherlock Holmes."

I looked at Holmes, shaking my head in disbelief.

For anyone who has never participated in the planning and opening of a new pub or restaurant, it is hard to understand just how much fun and laughter is experienced, whilst all the time running madly off in all directions. I found myself rushing my final patients out of the door at the end of the afternoons during that first week so that I could hurry back to 221B Baker Street and take part in the plans and laughter and interviews of the cooks, the *babushkas,* who had spent every day of the past thirty or more years of their lives in their kitchens, and who had so recently been forced to pack up and flee the pogroms and seek a better life in another country.

I could not help but feel profound admiration and respect for these women whose lives had so recently been turned upside down. In the midst of having to uproot themselves and their families, they managed to keep laughing and nattering endlessly about children and grandchildren and cooking. I could not understand a word they said since they sometimes spoke in Russian and usually in Yiddish. But the Countess, bless her, was accustomed to translating on the fly and in spite of her pretensions to the more elevated life, she treated her babushkas with respect and laughed along with them. Soon we had an entire regiment of cooks.

Then there were the barmaids, young strapping and beautiful *Natashas,* every one of them. The prospect of being paid every day for a day's work, no matter how hard and tiring, was one of the best things they could imagine. They were also expected to engage the male patrons in friendly if not entirely wholesome conversation with the goal of reporting their names and any data they could acquire to Holmes as soon as they returned to the confines of the kitchen.

The most curious of visitors to 221B were the score of Holmes's Baker Street Irregulars. Holmes was hiring them as busboys and dishwashers. I was fond of the lads, but I would have had no end of reservations about asking them to take on regimented gainful employment. The freedom of London's streets would be hard to leave behind, and I could not imagine that they would be prepared to arrive at set times every day and do their assigned tasks. I could only guess how long they would be stifled before they began to be truant.

I expressed my concerns to Holmes.

"Of course, they will chafe at their tethers," he replied. "But their assigned roles are only a guise for their true functions. I have told all of them that they are being hired as spies and that the jobs they do are merely their disguise. Every night, after The Balalaika closes its doors, each of them will be assigned to follow one of the customers and report on his place of abode. By the end of a fortnight, we will have a reasonably accurate preliminary list of every Russian immigrant whom we suspect might harbor anarchist tendencies. Wiggins had assured us that thirty Irregulars would be on duty every evening either giving service inside the pub or lurking around the doors ready to trail some departing patron to his home. For their efforts, they would receive a shilling a day. There was no end of boys applying for the positions."

By the end of the first week, the workers had all been chosen, and the center of activity shifted over to Spitalfields. Toiling through the night and into the wee small hours of the morning, hired tradesmen hung paintings, farm implements, and whatever the Slav equivalent was of *objets d'art*. Boxes arrived daily bearing colorful dresses and scarves, tea samovars, and more sacks of potatoes than I imagined an army could consume in a month.

I was curious concerning a small cubicle that carpenters were constructing behind the wall that separated the kitchen from the main eating and drinking room.

"That," said Holmes, "is our spy closet. There will be a very small opening, a sort of arrow slit, from which we shall be afforded a view of the patrons without their seeing us. We shall take turns secreting ourselves there and taking note of the patrons. I have no doubt that our anarchists will pay us a visit within the first week or so."

The Russian publisher that Holmes had been referred to by his brother, Mycroft, while useless as an informant, proved useful as our propagandist. His small local newspaper, published in both Russian and Yiddish, ran ads announcing the grand opening of The Balalaika in the heart of Spitalfields. Handbills were distributed and posted and included a short listing of the menu of food and drink that would become available.

And then, to top it all off, a group of musicians arrived and, in the midst of the whizzing and buzzing, began to practice their repertoire. It transformed the entire building into a place of laughter and jolliness. It was going swimmingly until the Wednesday of the second week.

Holmes and I had been up and out of 221B Baker Street at dawn so that we could arrive at our new establishment before the workmen did. I had canceled my appointments for the day and planned to join the fellows in swinging a hammer or piloting a paintbrush. Within an hour after we arrived, the tradesmen, the cooks, the Irregulars who had been recruited as busboys, the young Russian girls who had been hired as barmaids, and the dominating Countess were all on the premises and acting loudly.

At seven o'clock, through the door strode Inspector Lestrade, accompanied by Inspectors Gregson and Hopkins. Several of the tradesmen knew immediately who they were and you could hear a quiet buzz go through the room as eyeballs were suspiciously turned upon the visitors and quickly turned away again.

The three members of the Yard sat down at a table and beckoned one of the barmaids to come over to them. She nodded her understanding and said something in Russian and hastened into the kitchen. A minute later Sherlock Holmes emerged and gestured to me to join him as he approached the police officers.

"Ah, gentleman," he said, "how delightful to see you. I assure you that we are abiding by every rule and regulation that has been promulgated by the powers that be, so allow me to offer to bribe you with a generous serving of borsht and the finest imported vodka available anywhere on this sceptered isle. I do believe that is the standard practice between publicans and police officers in this district, is it not? I know it is still very early in the morning, but what is an uncivilized hour between friends?"

"Holmes, sit down," said Lestrade, "and cut out the nonsense. You know bloody well we did not come here as pub inspectors."

We sat down, and Holmes continued. "Very well, then. How might I be of assistance to not one but three esteemed inspectors from Scotland Yard this fine morning?"

"There's been another murder," said Lestrade. "Another Russian. And seeing as you, Holmes, have already stuck your nose into one murdered Russian and another attempted, I am putting you on this case as well. So kindly fetch your coat and hat and come with us."

Holmes visibly stiffened. "I beg your pardon, Inspector Lestrade, but as a private citizen, I am not in the habit of running and fetching for Scotland Yard. And as you can see, I am frightfully busy with my new enterprise. I have decided to become a publican."

Lestrade burst into laughter, as did Gregson and Hopkins, and, I must confess that I could not help myself from chuckling along with them.

"Right. Of course, you are, Holmes. And I am the Queen of Sheba. So, allow me to assist your latest enterprise. There are two hundred and sixty cases of vodka sitting on the excise dock, waiting to be shipped to this pub. Now, it would not be a good thing at all for your new calling as a publican if those cases were somehow not cleared for delivery until two weeks after your pub opens, now would it."

Lestrade sat back in his chair, crossed his arms over his chest, and smiled smugly. Holmes glared at him in anger, but then, as if admitting defeat, he forced a smile.

"Excuse me whilst I retrieve my coat and hat and I do believe I heard you say that my shipment would be delivered here by police carriage by the end of this afternoon, did I not?"

Lestrade grinned back at Holmes. "Yes, Holmes, I do believe I said that and Inspector Hopkins was about to leave us and look after that spot of business."

He gave a nod to Hopkins. "You know where we will be, right, Hopkins?"

"Shall see you there, shortly," said Hopkins.

The police carriage rattled and blasted its horn, bullying our way through the morning hustle and bustle of the London streets. We drove south to the Thames and then along the course of the Embankment towards Westminster. As we traveled, Lestrade stated such data as he had been given so far.

"We had a note from the head maid three hours ago. She found the victim in his bed when she brought in morning tea."

"No sounds of a struggle during the night?" interrupted Holmes.

"None, or at least that is what we were told. She found him lying on his back with a dagger in his heart. His body was already cold by the time we arrived, so it must have happened around midnight. Nothing appears to have been stolen or disturbed in the room. The fellow who was murdered goes by the name of Count Peter Vronsky. Now, we assume that he changed his name from *Pyotr* to *Peter* when he came to live in London."

"Are you referring to the Count Vronsky who lives off of Chester Square?" asked Holmes.

"Yes, that's the chap. You know him?"

"I know *of* him," said Holmes. "He is a widower and speaks with a distinct Russian accent."

"Right, and I assume you know that he is a distant member of the Romanov tribe. That connection is what done him in. On his chest, right beside the dagger, we found this."

He handed a scrap of paper of Holmes. There were two words in Cyrillic letters which Holmes, to my surprise, read.

"Narodnaya Volya."

"That's the same bunch of anarchists as before, right?" said Lestrade.

"It is indeed the same name," said Holmes.

Lestrade chattered on about what little data he had on the staff and other family members, and soon we arrived at a large, elegant, white terraced house that looked out onto Chester Square. There were several constables standing on the sidewalk and a small crowd of curious neighbors. I expected that the Press would soon be swarming the area.

The entrance hallway of the house was elegantly adorned and dominated by a large painting of Her Majesty. There was one of those hollow suits of armor in the corner that are so favored by the *nouveau riche,* along with some paintings of sunrises, haystacks, train stations, picnickers, and scenes of the Seine and the Eiffel Tower. They were all in that smudgy style, so beloved recently by the French. The presence of French *objets d'arte* seemed out of place until I recalled that that native tongue of the Royal Court in St. Petersburg was French. I permitted myself a brief moment of personal amusement, thinking how ironic it was that having valiantly defended themselves against Napoleon's army, the Russian Empire had surrendered to Paris's *flaneurs* and *artistes.*

My reverie was cut short as we entered the bed chamber and I gazed at the body lying supine across the bed. The dead Count was a man in his sixties, a few inches shorter than me, and was dressed informally, with his tie and jacket removed and his waistcoat unbuttoned.

Holmes stopped just after entering the room and before examining the body.

"Your men have already trampled the carpet, Inspector, removing any possible clues that might have been present there, but I do hope that nothing else has been disturbed."

"Nothing, Holmes. We are not complete imbeciles, even if you would like to believe we are."

"I assure you, Inspector, that I have never claimed that you were complete imbeciles," replied Holmes, with a very slight stress on the word *complete*.

He stood in place and gazed around the room. It was quite elegantly furnished and there were numerous paintings on the wall. Several were of the family of the late, lamented Czar of Russia, and there was yet another one of the well-known onion-domed church in Moscow. The remainder were scenes of the green hills and sheep. On the far wall from the head of the bed was a fine painting of the ominous Cliffs of Mohr. It appeared that this Count had not only been enamored of the French but also of the simple life of the common Irish shepherd.

Holmes also looked over the room but did not appear to give much interest to the paintings.

"Was the window open when you arrived?" he asked Lestrade.

"It was," said Lestrade. "We asked about that first thing, and the maid said that she had not opened it. It was ajar when she entered."

"And the furniture was in the same place as it is now?"

"Nothing has been moved, Holmes."

"Very well. Kindly allow me a few minutes to conduct my inspection."

"We were fully expecting you to do just that," said Lestrade.

Without being asked, I took out my notebook and followed Holmes around the room. He took a close look at the open window, and at the bookcase and writing desk, and then in the man's clothes closet. Finally, having examined the room itself, he moved over to the body. There was a dagger, inserted all the way to the hilt into the man's left pectoral muscle and some blood had spread to the white shirt.

Using his glass, Holmes then carefully examined the poor fellow's neck and requested that I raise the body to sitting position so that he could look carefully at the other side of his head, his neck, and his back.

He then turned to Inspector Lestrade.

"Permit me to ask, Inspector, if you have reached any conclusions about what took place here?"

"It seems a bit straightforward. There are jewels and quite the hoard of banknotes in the drawers of the writing desk and not at all disturbed. So that rules out robbery. The window was open, and it would not be difficult to place a ladder against the wall and climb in and stab the fellow. He's not a very big chap, so anyone who was fast, like that fellow we chased in Kensington for example, could have popped in, quickly stabbed the Count, pushed him back on the bed as he staggered ... or maybe he staggered all by himself ... and then jumped back out the window faster than a buttered bullet. So it looks to us like it was another assassination by those anarchist chaps. Seeing as you appear to be building a pub with the plan of trapping them there, you better add this murder to your list."

"Ah, Inspector, I congratulate you on having discerned my motive in becoming a publican. On that score, you batted a century. Well done."

"We were not born yesterday, Holmes. Now, do you think it was the same chap as did in Count Myshkin in the hospital, or took a shot at the Prince and Duchess?"

"Ah, my dear inspector, I said that you were right on my reasons for opening a new pub, but I regret to inform you that on every other conclusion you were wrong."

Lestrade looked annoyed and nonplussed. "Explain yourself, Holmes. It looks like a stabbing plain and simple to me, and happened just like I said."

"Doctor," said Holmes, turning to me. "Kindly remind Inspector Lestrade how long a heart keeps pumping blood after it has stopped beating."

The question was nonsensical, and I shook my head. "When it stops beating, it stops pumping blood, of course."

"Indeed, but until it stops and a deep cut has been made into the torso, how much blood can one expect to see?"

"Quite abundant amounts. More or less depending on if an artery or major vein has been severed."

"Precisely. And how much blood is on the man's shirt and bedclothes?"

"Hardly any," I said. "Why then, he must have been dead already before he was stabbed."

"Precisely, unless we suppose that the murderer cleaned up all the blood and put a clean shirt on his victim before leaving. I am sure, Inspector, that you do not think your anarchist paused for that reason."

Lestrade did not answer the question and glared back at Holmes. "Just keep going, Holmes. Get on with it."

"There are bruises on the neck. There is one on each side of the Adam's Apple and eight smaller bruises on the back of the neck. You may recall, doctor, that on the day you met me, I had been studying the duration of time after death that a body was capable of forming bruises."

"I do indeed recall, and the bruises cease to appear almost immediately after death."

"Correct. Therefore, it is obvious that the man was strangled to death, and the dagger inserted as an afterthought with the intent of diverting us. Now, if you will examine the writing desk closely, you will see that while the cash and jewels are undisturbed, the small stack of stationary is somewhat out of order, and the paper on which the note is written is of exactly the same character as the victim's stationary."

"Right," said Lestrade. "So, the fellow hops in the window, strangles the Count with his bare hands, then writes a note and finally plunges a dagger into him to lead us down the wrong path."

"That is an improvement on your previous effort, Inspector, but not yet correct."

"Oh, very well then, Holmes. Get on with it. We don't have all morning."

"Nor do I, sir. So, kindly direct your attention to the window sill and sash. If a man entered through that window, the fine layer of dust would have been extensively disturbed. But it has not been. There are only two sets of markings, one on the left-hand sash and one on the sill. Both consist of four short rows of smudges."

"From a hand," I interjected.

"Precisely, but it is a small hand, too small to belong to an adult male. And, if I am not mistaken, there is a faint scent of perfume in this room. I believe the particular brand is *Milles Fleurs*, although I cannot make that claim for certain."

"A woman?" gasped Lestrade. "But how could a woman have strangled a grown man? That is preposterous."

"My dear Inspector, I did not say that a woman committed the murder, only that a woman was present in the room during or before the murder. Obviously, the murder was committed by a man, and a rather powerful one at that."

"Ah ha," said Lestrade. "So, there is a female amongst the anarchists. Yes, I can see it all now. Being ruthless and shameless, she must have seduced the Count and gained access to his bed chamber and once there opened the window and gestured to her male accomplice. He then slipped into the house, opened the door to this room, which she must have left unlocked, and overpowered the Count. After he had killed him, he wrote out the note in Russian and stabbed him for good measure. Yes, yes. He wanted to send a message to all the Russian nobility that their days were numbered. You would agree, would you not Holmes, that that is what must have happened here?"

Holmes sighed and smiled at Lestrade in a most condescending manner.

"Congratulations, Inspector. You have deduced correctly on perhaps one-quarter of the matter. The remaining three-quarters is entirely wrong. However, before enlightening you, may I ask if the household staff has been sequestered and required to remain on the premises? It is imperative that I speak with them immediately. Oh, and on your way out, you might glance at the bookcase and see which of the volumes is not aligned properly with the rest of them."

I had been thinking along the same lines as Inspector Lestrade. The only difference between him and me was that I had learned not to be surprised and disappointed when Holmes, with barely concealed arrogance, dismissed my conclusions. The poor inspector had not yet acquired that skill, and the look on his face betrayed both his anger and quandary.

"What ...?' he mumbled and gave a quick glance to the bookcase. "Oh, very well Holmes, if you must play games with me, go ahead. The staff are all gathered in the library. None has been permitted to leave the premises. You can go and cross-question them, but then I demand an explanation of what you just said."

"Why, of course, Inspector. I would never dream of failing to enlighten you."

Holmes, Inspectors Gregson and Lestrade and I descended the stairs and entered the library. There must have been a dozen staff present, as would be expected for the management of a well-heeled city dwelling. Inspector Hopkins had arrived and stood at the door, barring any from leaving, but none seemed to be overly distraught by the events of the morning, and they were all chatting amiably amongst themselves.

Holmes spoke quietly to Hopkins who, in turn, spoke to the staff.

"Your attention here now. Listen to this. Each of you is to stand, one at a time, and state your name and position in the Count's household."

As instructed, each member stood spoke out accordingly. We passed, in no particular order except as to where they had been seated, through the butler, the housekeeper, the various maids, footmen, a bookkeeper, a driver, grooms, cooks, page, and gardeners.

I had known Sherlock Holmes long enough and well enough to suspect that he had good reason for wanting to meet the entire household staff. Except for the driver and the page, the males on staff were all built, as we used to say in the Fusiliers, like brick privies. They were stocky fellows and whilst they did not look or speak like foreigners, seemed like chaps who were not to be trifled with unless one wished to end up being badly knocked about. The driver was tall and lean and the page likewise thin but, being young, much shorter.

Holmes then proceeded to move slowly around the room, greeting each of the staff by name and confirming their position. He extended his hand to each of them, bowing graciously to the women, who remained seated, and smiling to the men and boys, who stood and shook his hand.

When he had completed the task, he turned to Inspector Lestrade and gesturing to the man who had identified himself as the driver, said, "Inspector, arrest this man for the murder of Count Vronsky."

A look of shock and then panic swept across the driver's face. He jumped to his feet and in several strides of his long legs attempted to flee the room. Hopkins and Gregson tackled him and wrestled him to the ground and held him fast while Lestrade, after some understandable hesitation, snapped on a set of handcuffs.

"He had it coming!" the man was shouting. "He had it coming. He was evil, I tell you, evil!"

He kept up his shouts as the two stalwart members of Scotland Yard led him away.

Once the fellow had been led out of the room and toward the police carriage, Holmes stepped across the room until he was standing in front of the young woman who had identified herself as the bookkeeper. She was pale and visibly trembling.

"Miss," said Holmes. "I suggest that you join your brother and give your story to the Inspectors. I have no doubt that his actions were arguably justified. Are you able to walk to the carriage or do you need assistance?"

"No," she said is a whisper. "I will be all right."

She stood and, after taking a deep breath to compose herself, left the room.

"Nobody leaves here yet," ordered Lestrade. Then turning to Holmes, said, "Go and sit in the front parlor, Holmes. I need an explanation."

Holmes smiled and bowed, and the two of us found our way to the front room.

"Right, now start talking," said Lestrade as he entered and took a seat.

"And where might you like me to begin?" asked Holmes.

"Just begin," snapped Lestrade. "You know what I need to know."

"Indeed, I do," said Holmes. "Very well then, to begin with, the dead man's name is not Count Vronsky. He is no more a Russian noble than you or I are. His name is Peter O'Gorman, and he hails from somewhere outside of Dublin. Thirty years ago, he became connected with some Russian traders and secured the rights to import Russian goods – sable, vodka, caviar, lumber, minerals and the like – into England and to send many fine English products back to the Russians. He became exceptionally wealthy. But, being Irish, he was excluded from all the fine clubs and gatherings in London, so he cleverly adopted the identity of a Russian noble, a distant member of the Czar's family. He disguised his Irish tongue by affecting a thick Russian accent and mannerisms and was duly welcomed into the society of English bluebloods, as anyone of noble birth and royal blood always is.

"He claimed that his wife had died many years ago, although it is possible that he abandoned her in Ireland. It is likely that she was of decent Catholic stock and had no interest in participating in his pretense, although that is mere conjecture. You will need to locate her if she exists, as she would be in line to inherit a small fortune."

"We can deal with his wife later," said Lestrade. "Get on with how you knew who the murderer was."

"Oh, yes ... that. Did you happen to observe the bookshelf, as I had suggested.?"

"You know bloody well I did not. I followed you out of the room straight away."

"Yes, of course. I do recall that. Well, had you taken a moment to do so you would have observed that all of the books were perfectly lined up on the shelf except for one. That one was an English – Russian dictionary. The perfect placing of all of the books and everything else in the room, and the house for that matter, indicated that Mr. O'Gorman was more than somewhat obsessive about neatness and order. If a single book were out of place, he would have put it back where it exactly belonged, forthwith. Someone, most likely the murderer, had used it to confirm the translation and Cyrillic spelling of *People's Will*. The fact that there was an error in the Cyrillic letters was also a telltale clue.

"What appears to have happened is that the young woman, the bookkeeper, had been summoned to the man's bedchamber and was being indecently assaulted. She managed to push the window open and signal to the driver, who is her older brother, that she was in distress. He bounded up into the house and into the room and, seeing what was taking place, in a fit of rage, strangled the man. One can never condone murder, but there are at least some mitigating circumstances that should come out in court and save him from the gallows."

"But how," I asked, "did you know which one it was? Any one of those men in the library could have overpowered the Count, or whoever he was."

"The tall one," said Holmes and said no more.

"Holmes," said Lestrade. "Get over your smugness and get on with it. How did you know?"

Holmes gave a subtle roll of his eyes and affected a sigh. "Kindly observe."

He stood and beckoned to me.

"My dear doctor, please bend your knees so that you significantly shorten your stature and then grasp me around the neck as if you were strangling me."

I stood and did what he had asked, reaching my arms upward toward his throat and placing my hands around it.

"Excellent. Now, Inspector, please note the position of Doctor Watson's thumbs on the front of my neck relative to the position of his four fingers on the back. You will see that his thumb lines up with the position of his smallest finger. Do you see that, Inspector?"

"I do. What of it?"

"Excellent. Now we will reverse our relative statures, and I will become much shorter than the doctor. He will again place his hands in a position as if to strangle me."

I extended my legs and Holmes dipped his knees until he was a full foot shorter than me. I again placed my hands on his neck, and he turned once more to Lestrade.

"Now, Inspector, you will see that when the man grabbing the neck is much taller than his victim, and reaching down, the thumb on the front of the neck becomes aligned with the index finger on the back of the neck. Thank you, doctor, that is good enough. It seems that Inspector Lestrade now understands."

"So, you chose the tall one," said the Inspector. "What if there had been two or three tall ones. Then you would have been in a spot."

"Perhaps, except that the likelihood of two or three all having fresh cuts and bruises on their hands and wrists, placed there in desperation by a man who was being strangled, would have been highly unlikely."

Lestrade harrumphed. "As soon as you addressed the woman as his sister, I could see the family resemblance."

"Indeed, it was impossible to miss it. Did you also notice the bruises on her wrists? No? Pity. They were rather hard to miss. Is there anything else you need to know, Inspector? If not, we really are frightfully busy and must get back to Spitalfields."

Holmes and I rose and departed the house in Belgravia and hailed a cab back across the city. He is usually somewhat voluble after solving a case so quickly and, frankly, a bit full of himself. This time, however, he was silent. He had leaned back into the seat and closed his eyes. Knowing that he had no interest in conversation, I said nothing and contented myself to peer out of the cab window as we drove through Westminster and along the Embankment. That lasted until we had just passed Blackfriars.

"You are quite right," he said quietly. "She did not seem the type."

"No, she did not at all," I responded. Then I startled.

"Really, Holmes, I would rather that my mind were a private place. *Must* you do that to me?"

"Must I? Not at all, I assure you it is entirely voluntary." He smiled warmly and laughed at me.

"This time there was no war wound or gazing at pictures on the wall involved. You could not have been more obvious had you sent a telegraph. I merely observed you staring at several young women who were on the pavement as we passed. Most were passably attractive, for English girls, but when we passed one who was decidedly unattractive, you shook your head. You had the same thought as I had. You were thinking that the singularly unattractive bookkeeper was not the type who would normally inflame the uncontrolled passions of a sixty-year-old man, even if he did come from Dublin. That was what you were thinking, was it not?"

"Yes, it was. I confess. I never want to allow myself to be uncharitable in my thoughts towards the fairer sex, but there was a half dozen or more buxom beauties on his staff, and it made no sense that he would choose the homeliest. What did you make of that?"

"I make of it nothing at all, yet. But it does provide a piece of data that is incongruous with the rest of the picture."

He closed his eyes again and stayed that way until we were almost back at The Balalaika.

There was one other question that was burning in my mind that I just had to ask.

"How in heaven's name could you have known all those facts about the Count? Even the police and his staff did not appear to know his true identity."

"Coincidentally, I only learned about him recently. The Countess, who in some ways resembles him, had told me about him."

"Indeed? Why?"

"Because he is not only an agent for importing Russian vodka and caviar into London, he is *our* agent, and if we cannot replace him, our success in running a fine establishment here in Spitalfields will be very limited and short."

"That is a curious coincidence, I must say," I said.

"My dear doctor, when dealing with criminal enterprises, coincidences are extremely rare."

Chapter Eight

They All Love the Balalaika

The remaining few days until the opening of The Balalaika were a beehive of activity. I thought that we would never be ready to serve food and drink to eager customers, but on the final morning, as I walked through the full three floors of the building, I could not help but smile at what had been accomplished. I had never been to the great steppes of the Ukraine or set foot inside the Pale of Settlement, and had no desire ever to do so. But if a splendid eatery and pub might have existed in those distant places, then it surely would have resembled The Balalaika in Spitalfields, London.

By three o'clock in the afternoon, the cooks had already prepared many of the dishes they expected to serve. The barmaids were all in place and costumed to look like pretty peasant girls from the banks of the Don, howbeit with bodices cut somewhat, perhaps brazenly, lower than any *babushka* would have permitted. Bottles of vodka sat on every table, adjacent to bowls of wedges of fresh tomatoes, ready to be consumed. At half-past three I noticed customers lining up outside the door. By four-thirty the line stretched around the corner of the building and down the block.

At five o'clock, the Countess threw open the doors and in a loud and boisterous voice invited all and sundry inside. Within a few minutes, well over one hundred men and a smaller number of women had entered and claimed their places on the barstools and at the tables. On the ground floor, a line formed immediately at the bar, where orders for food and drink were placed and filled as quickly as possible. The second floor offered table service and the large room on the third floor was left vacant, to be used for future lectures, recitals, and other events.

The barmaids, waiters, and Irregulars all hustled about taking and delivering orders and clearing tables, but they had all been instructed to report back to the kitchen and inform Sherlock Holmes and Inspector Gregson of any names of customers they might catch and topics of conversation overheard. I was assigned to the small cabinet with the viewing slit that allowed me to observe unseen with the hope that I might catch a glimpse of the fellow who had escaped my clutches in the hospital. Holmes had also recruited both the orderly and the floor nurse to take turns with me for the same task. They were delighted with the additional income and seemed to be enjoying the camaraderie that took place behind the kitchen doors.

Any characters that aroused our suspicions were followed discretely to their abodes by an Irregular or a bobby in plain clothes after departing from The Balalaika.

All went swimmingly for the first week. The atmosphere in our pub was joyful and convivial. The vodka flowed freely amidst endless toasts. The musicians played well, or at least sufficiently well after three vodka toasts by their listeners, and were cheered on. For hundreds of young people who had so recently been forced to flee their homes following such vicious persecution, it offered a joyful respite from the tragedies they had suffered. Jokes and songs carried on in Yiddish, German, Polish and several languages that I could not possibly identify. The Countess assured me that within a month we would have recovered our investment and turned a healthy profit.

Meanwhile, Holmes and the Yard had compiled a list of over fifty shady characters, complete with their names and places of residence. But as of yet, no sign whatsoever of our anarchist assassin.

Several days later, I rose in the morning and made my way to our front room, eagerly looking forward to yet another fine breakfast Mrs. Hudson had prepared for us. I was surprised to find that Holmes, Lestrade, and Gregson were all assembled around the table, with sheets of paper occupying the place at which I had hoped to soon find my food. Holmes merely gesticulated to an empty cup and the pot of coffee and continued to look at the pages in front of him. Over his shoulder, I could see that they held the lists of names and addresses and some additional observations of the fellows who had aroused their suspicions.

"Are you," I asked, "distilling the list into a smaller group of the usual suspects?"

Holmes put down the page he was looking at and sat back.

"We still need much more data, but there were three chaps that struck us as highly interesting. Here, look at the notes on these fellows."

I looked at the paper he held out to me. On it were the names of three men as reported by one of the barmaids. There was no last name, but they addressed each other as Dimitri, Ivan, and Alyosha and appeared to be brothers.

"Obviously," I said, having clearly deduced the illusion, "these are fictional names. Even I can see that. They must be trying to disguise their true identities."

"Watson," said Holmes, "could you please use your God-given brain for something more than stating what a school-child could see. Will you please look at the address to which they were followed?"

Feeling somewhat abashed, I looked again at the page.

"Ah, ha. They are not just poor immigrants living in the slums of Spitalfields. This address is in Belgravia. These chaps are connected somehow to a higher level of society."

Again, Holmes sighed in condescension. "The specific address. What is it?"

"It is on Chester Square. Why, that is quite close to the place where your Russian Count from Ireland lived, is it not?"

"No, Watson. It is not 'quite close.' It is the exact same address."

Later that afternoon, I hurried over to The Balalaika and resumed my post in the cabinet, observing the patrons and trying to spot our assassin. At the end of the evening, I concluded that it was a hopeless task.

"Holmes," I said, "you have invited the entire mass of Russian immigrants, Jews, Catholics, Orthodox and atheists alike. We are inundated with young foreigners of all possible persuasions. How will you possibly single out your anarchist in this crowd? It has been impossible."

"We have no choice but to attract a large crowd of customers if we are not to bankrupt the effort. But beginning next Friday evening, our humble pub will become a revolutionary salon and will be the host of a spirited political debate. We shall make use of the spacious third floor, and two willing professors from London University have agreed to debate each other on the topic of *Who is the Superior Revolutionary Thinker? Mikail Bakumin or Pyotr Kropotkin?* I am quite certain that every self-respecting Russian anarchist in London will be here."

"But," I protested, "we will still be overrun by all those young immigrants."

'No, my dear doctor. You were not listening. I said that we would hold the event on Friday evening."

I was in a fog as to what he could possibly be saying, but then the light dawned.

"Oh, yes. Of course," I said. "All the observant Jews will be with their families."

"Precisely. Leaving us with only the *goyim*, among whom we shall have good prospects to find our would-be assassins. As you clearly observed one of them, it is essential that you be there, in disguise, of course. The Irregulars who hit the chap with the stone and chased him through Kensington Gardens will also be present. I have also sent a note to Dr. Trevelyan asking if he could join us for the evening as he had by far the most open encounters with our prey. Scotland Yard will also have a few of their sturdier constables lurking outside to apprehend the villain once we identify him. I have reasonable certainty that we have good odds of enticing the fellow and entrapping him."

It seemed to me to be a promising plan, or at least the most promising advanced to date. Therefore, on that Friday, I terminated my patients' visits at four o'clock and made my way by cab as quickly as I could to Spitalfields.

As had become our custom, we opened the doors at five o'clock, and the huddled masses entered, yearning for their *stoli* and *blini*. I had deliberately not shaved for the past three days, had added a theatrical mustache that Holmes had kindly provided for me, and donned my poorest looking attire, all in an attempt to pass for a middle-aged English member of a radical organization or a trade union. I had not read any of the appropriate texts that would be the subject of the debate, but I had read reviews of them in *The Times*, which, I suspected, was more than most of the attendees had done.

I had not, however, acquired the intestinal fortitude to drink cheap vodka straight out of the bottle, so I ordered a Guinness and sat at a table where other gentlemen of my ilk were speaking English. Two of them were attempting to impress the table with their erudition by quoting Marx and Engels, but after two rounds of ale, we settled into s spirited discussion of the past weekend's football match and friendly arguments as to which of Everton or Blackburn would triumph at the end of the season.

At half past six, the Countess made an announcement that the door of the third-floor room had been opened and that those interested in participating in the debate were welcome to take their places. About a third of the assembled customers rose and began to move to the stairwell. I saw several reach for the bottle of vodka and slide it underneath their jackets as they departed from the tables in the pub.

As I climbed the stairs, a stooped, elderly chap with matted gray hair and a worn working man's cap hobbled up alongside me. He was obviously having difficulty with the steps, and I held my forearm out to offer him some stability. With an asthmatic wheeze, he gasped and thanked me. A few steps later he nearly toppled backward, and I was forced to pull his body close to me. At that point, he leaned his head very close to mine, and I heard a familiar voice whisper in my ear.

"My dear Watson, you are always such a considerate Christian gentleman."

I merely rolled my eyes and loosened my grip.

Chapter Nine

The Best Laid Plans

We took our seats in what had been converted into a lecture hall. Unlike the talk I had attended several weeks ago at the splendid new Natural History Museum — the event that had started this increasingly complicated case — the crowd was not composed of the well-dressed cream of London intelligentsia, but of the common proletariat. Their having had two hours to consume copious amounts of vodka before gathering for the debate contributed to the volume of the voices, and I anticipated a lively evening.

The room was filling up and, on several occasions, I noticed Holmes glancing at his watch.

"We are running on schedule, are we not?" I asked.

"Yes, but I had asked Dr. Trevelyan to be present and to arrive before the doors opened. He is the best equipped to identify the catatonic patient. But he has not shown up."

Just before the speakers were to be introduced, I felt a gentle elbow in my side from Holmes. With his eyes, he directed mine to the back corner of the room. There was a table there with six young men, all around the same age. They were dressed as members of the working class and were, unlike the tables around them, sitting quietly and engaging in subdued conversation.

"Can you get a close look," he asked, "at the man with his back toward us? Wait until he turns his head and tell me if you think he looks familiar."

I kept looking at the fellow Holmes had indicated and when, for a few brief moments, he turned his head and allowed me to see his profile, I gave a bump with my elbow back to Holmes.

"That's him," I whispered. "I cannot be entirely certain, but all of the men who have come and gone through this place so far, he is the only one that closely resembles the rascal that punched me in the face."

"Excellent. Please just wait here, and I will find Hopkins and alert him. If possible, we shall remove him from the premises without an undue commotion. A donnybrook would be bad for business."

Holmes stood and began to shuffle his way around me. He suddenly stopped, and I felt his hand clasp onto my shoulder. I looked up at him, and even through his disguise I could see a look of dismay spread across his face. He was staring at the door. I did likewise and saw Dr. Trevelyan sauntering through it, making no attempt at all to disguise himself or keep out of the sight of any of the chaps sitting in the room.

I held my breath as he crossed the front of the room and walked toward the door at the back of the stage area. What I feared would happen then did. The man whom Holmes and I had identified as the killer fixed his gaze directly on the doctor. For several seconds he sat, frozen and staring. Then he leapt to his feet and shouted.

"Eta lovushka! Ukhodi otsyuda! Beg!"

He had spotted the trap and he began running quickly toward the door, pushing everyone in the way out of his path. He was running directly along the aisle where Holmes and I were seated, and this time I was ready for him. Just as he was about to pass us, I jumped to my feet, took a hefty swing and landed a haymaker right on his jaw. He dropped to the ground, and I was ready to pounce on him when my eye caught the flash of a revolver barrel. My military instincts kicked in and I flung myself to the ground just as the gun fired. The bullet struck the glasses and bottles behind the bar, and the room erupted into pandemonium. Shout and screams were heard from every corner. Those near the doors rushed to exit. Our killer, nimble as a rabbit, leapt up onto the tables and sprinted across them, passing the other patrons and leaping through the door and down into the stairwell. I put my hand into my pocket and withdrew my service revolver and tried to force my way through the crowd to chase him, but to no avail.

"Stop him!" I shouted. "Police. Stop him!"

I could see Inspector Hopkins push his way through the mass of panicked men and women and run down the stairs, but I knew that our well-planned opportunity had vanished.

The Countess quickly exercised her voice at the volume of a foghorn and quelled the masses. The crowd slowly shuffled back to their seats, and the barmaids soon appeared with a fresh round of complimentary bottles of vodka. The debate commenced.

I have known Holmes well enough and long enough to read the disappointment that his bodily posture conveyed. After listening to the first speaker, he shook his head, stood up and shuffled toward the door. I followed him. Once we had reached the ground floor, he walked slowly back to the office rooms and sat down, dropping his head into his hands. I followed him into the room, and we sat in silence for a full twenty minutes. Then Inspector Lestrade, who had been stationed on the lower floor, entered the room and closed the door.

I stated what was already patently obvious.

"He got away?"

"He did," said Lestrade. "He did. Hopkins and several constables gave chase, but he was too fast for them. He headed right into the market and even at this hour it's still busy. We lost him."

"Were you able," said Holmes, lifting his head from his hands, "to interrogate any of those who were with him?"

"Oh, yes. We quietly removed them from the room, hauled them down a flight, and separated them. Gregson and a couple of constables put the thumbscrews to them, you might say. One of them sang and snitched on the rest. The fellow we were after goes by the name of Boris Drubetskoy. He is a member of the *Narodnaya Volya* and arrived here in London back in June. He was part of the cell that assassinated the Czar, and he was the one that tried to shoot the Duchess. That was him alright."

"How has he managed to evade the Okhrana?" asked Holmes. "They must have sent a file on him to Scotland Yard."

"We will investigate that issue, but from what the snitcher told us, our killer had a complete set of forged papers, as do at least a hundred others. And they have all come from the same source."

"Who?" I asked.

"It does not matter now," said Lestrade. "He's dead. But before being murdered, he seems to have supplied any anarchist who paid him with a false identity. I suppose we should have been able to spot the forgeries. He gave them all names from his favorite Russian novels. And he also appears to have supplied a certain Mr. Sherlock Holmes with over a hundred cases of vodka, to be consumed at The Balalaika."

For several seconds, Holmes did not reply and then he spoke.

"That does," he said, "put a rather different interpretation on his murder, does it not?"

"It does. The driver and his sister, who you thought was having her virtue defended by an enraged brother, are from Yorkshire although their parents came from Russia. But both were paid agents of the Okhrana. It seems that the Count may have deduced who they were and was about to kill the girl when her brother stormed in and saved her. But that also does not matter anymore. The Russian Embassy took them away,

111

claiming diplomatic immunity. They're on their way to St. Petersburg."

All three of us then sat back in our chairs and said no more. Our hours and hours of planning had been for naught. The expenses, the acquiring of the artifacts, the vodka, the food, the Natashas, the babushkas … all for naught. It had been a colossal waste of time. The killer had escaped a third time and was free to kill again. It was a dreadfully gloomy few minutes.

Holmes finally stood and in a subdued voice said, "I believe that I must get back to my chemistry experiments. Please, Inspector, extend my apologies to your colleagues at the Yard. I will, as a matter of principle, forfeit my fee. *Maintenant, il faut cultiver notre jardin.*"

His head bowed, he opened the door to leave the room and was stopped by a clatter and commotion in the hallway. Barging past him into the room strode a gaggle of half a dozen constables. In the middle of the pack, his wrists secured in handcuffs and with a large bobby firmly attached to each arm was the wiry, swarthy man that had recently been identified as Boris Drubetskoy. His face was bloodied, and he appeared dazed and confused.

"Good Lord!" exclaimed Lestrade. "you caught him. Well done, men. Well done!"

"This is him, i'n it?" said one of the constables. "We were not over sure, Inspector. We thought it was, but none of had the good look at his face. Only his back as he fled."

"Yes, yes, this is him," said Lestrade. "Would you agree, Holmes? This is him, is it not? Splendid, men, just splendid. Those stuffed shirts over at Whitehall will be happy as larks when they hear. So will the Russians at the Embassy. Splendid. Just jolly splendid. Well done, men. Well done."

"What shall we do with him, Inspector, sir?"

"Keep him firmly bound. He's a slippery one, he is. And take him to one of the cells at the Yard. Nobody talks to him until I get there. I shall come as soon as I have notified Whitehall. Really, my good men, this is entirely splendid."

I had never seen Inspector Lestrade so utterly giddy.

"Are you not, Inspector," said Holmes, "even going to do us the courtesy of asking the officer who apprehended him to give a report?"

"Oh, yes, I suppose so, yes. Yes. I suppose a quick report would be in order. Which of you fine fellows caught this dangerous fellow and took him down?"

"That would have been me, sir," said one of the constables stepping forward.

"Was it now?" said Lestrade. "Constable Simmons, right? Well then, Simmons, very well done my good man. A citation shall most likely be forthcoming. Did he fire his gun at you as he did in the pub? Were you wounded or injured in any way? I must say, you are indeed a brave and courageous officer. Just the type we are proud to have as a member of London's finest."

"Well sir, that is all right and kind of you, but it were not quite like that."

"No. Well then, what happened? Give us a quick report," said Lestrade.

"It were a bit strange, sir. We chased him from the corner right up and into the market, but he were fast, sir. There were no way we were going to catch him. Once he was in the market, it being Friday evening and all, and all the stalls being open and such, well, we knew we had lost him. And we knew that it were hopeless to go on looking for him in the crowd, but we circulated back and forth asking the folks and the merchants in the stalls if they had seen any chap fitting his description and all they could do is say yes, any one of a hundred people in the market fit his description. So, we knew it were hopeless, like I said, sir."

"Go on, Simmons. Go on. What happened?"

"Well, Inspector, sir, I were in the fishmongers section and this woman, one of the fishmonger's wives, comes up to me and grabs my arm and looks like she needs a policeman right urgent. Being as we were looking for the killer, I didn't want to get distracted with anything else, sir. So, I tried to tell her to wait a while. But she were insistent, and she says I have to come right sharp to the next aisle because a man might be dying there. So, I decided that were a good enough reason to leave what I knew were a hopeless task anyway, and I go over to her stall and there, lying on the floor, out cold he was, is the chap we were chasing. Or at least it looks like him, and the clothes were the same.

"So, I give a good blast on my whistle and the rest of my mates come running and we think that it's our man, all right, lying on the floor with his lights out. So, we snapped the cuffs on him and got some cold water and bring him around and brought him here."

"I can see," said Lestrade, "that you brought him here. You don't have to tell me that. But what happened?"

"Well sir, I asked the fish lady that same question, and she says that she and her husband were standing in their stall just doing their selling as usual, sir, and they see this chap walking past, all nonchalant and minding his own business and such. Then out of nowhere, she says, a rock comes flying at his head, bonks him a good one, and he drops like a stone to the floor. She is all upset because they don't like no violence in the market, it not being good for business and all. So, she give chase to the culprit but he ran off, and all she could tell me about him is that he were a fat little urchin."

Such were the singular circumstances in connection with the impatient dissidents and anarchists that all began with the doctor from King's College. After that night at The Balalaika, the heads of the anarchist organization in England were removed but others grew in their place. Most did not remain in Britain and it is surmised at Scotland Yard that many of them joined the passengers on the ships taking immigrants to America, while others slowly made their way back to Russia, determined to carry on the quest to destroy the rule of the Czar. I remain hopeful that that great country will continue to evolve into a modern, peaceful nation. Sherlock Holmes does not share my optimism.

Dear Sherlockian Reader:

The original story in the Canon, *The Adventure of the Resident Patient*, ascribed to the elderly mute gentleman the identify of a Russian nobleman. That was enough of a cue to me to pick up on the influx of Russians to London during the final years of the 19th Century and the early years of the 20th. Researching the story led me to learn the following:

The historical setting of this story starts with the cluster of events that took place in Eastern Europe during the 1880s: the assassination of the Czar by a group of anarchists, the retaliatory pogroms against the Jews throughout the Pale of Settlement, and the subsequent mass emigration of millions of Jews from Eastern Europe and into the West. Most of them ended up in the United States of America, but many also moved to England, France, Canada, Australia, South Africa and other parts of Western Europe and South America — the Diaspora. The most familiar story of that time is likely the great musical, *Fiddler on the Roof.*

Throughout the last two decades of the 1800s and up to the outbreak of the Great War, there were many radical and anarchist writers and related movements across Europe. Their activities often accomplished nothing but, ultimately, they took over power in Russia in 1917 and the world was never the same after.

The cover has a picture of the young Lenin. He was not part of the Narodnaya Volya, but his older brother, Aleksandr Ilyich Ulyanov, was and participated in the attempted assassination Czar Alexander III in 1887 and was caught and executed. The Bolshevik movement and the development of global communism grew out of these movements.

The activities of the Narodnaya Volya in England are fictional.

Spitalfields and the Spitalfields Market area were the part of London in which many immigrant groups first settled. The Huguenots settled there in the 1700s and the Jews from Eastern Europe made their homes there in the late 1800s. Spitalfields Market is still in operation today.

The Ten Bells Pub has been close to the Spitalfields Market for a very long time. Two of the prostitutes who plied their trade from that pub, Mary Kelly and Annie Chapman, were among the women murdered by Jack the Ripper in 1888. The pub is still in operation today, having changed its name to the Jack the Ripper Pub and then back to Ten Bells. The Christ Church Spitalfields also still stands across the road from the pub.

Prince Alfred, the second son of Queen Victoria, had a distinguished career in the Royal Navy and married Grand Duchess Maria, daughter of the Czar of Russia. An attempt was made on his life when he visited Australia, but none thereafter.

The mental disorder that we now know today at Post Traumatic Stress Disorder, or PTSD, was originally identified during and following the American Civil War and the Boer Wars. At that time, it was called *Soldier's Heart* because it was observed in soldiers who had been in active battle and the most common symptom was an elevated heartbeat. In the years and wars that followed, it was also called shell shock or battle fatigue. In Victorian England, it was devastating to those who suffered from it. It still is today.

Thank you for reading this New Sherlock Holmes Mystery. Hope you enjoyed it.

Warm regards,

Craig

About the Author

In May of 2014 the Sherlock Holmes Society of Canada – better known as The Bootmakers – announced a contest for a new Sherlock Holmes story. Although he had no experience writing fiction, the author submitted a short Sherlock Holmes mystery and was blessed to be declared one of the winners. Thus inspired, he has continued to write new Sherlock Holmes Mysteries since and is on a mission to write a new story as a tribute to each of the sixty stories in the original Canon. He has been writing these stories while living in Toronto, the Okanagan Valley, Buenos Aires, Bahrain, and Manhattan.

New Sherlock Holmes Mysteries
by Craig Stephen Copland

www.SherlockHolmesMystery.com

"Best selling series of new Sherlock Holmes stories. All faithful to The Canon."

This is the first book in the series. Go to my website, start with this one and enjoy MORE SHERLOCK.

Studying Scarlet. Starlet O'Halloran, a fabulous mature woman, who reminds the reader of Scarlet O'Hara (but who, for copyright reasons cannot actually be her) has arrived in London looking for her long-lost husband, Brett (who resembles Rhett Butler, but who, for copyright reasons, cannot actually be him). She enlists the help of Sherlock Holmes. This is an unauthorized parody, inspired by Arthur Conan Doyle's *A Study in Scarlet* and Margaret Mitchell's *Gone with the Wind*.

Six new Sherlock Holmes stories are always free to enjoy. If you have not already read them, go to this site, sign up, download and enjoy. www.SherlockHolmesMystery.com

Super Collections A, B and C

57 New Sherlock Holmes Mysteries.

The perfect ebooks for readers who subscribe to Kindle Unlimited

Enter 'Craig Stephen Copland Sherlock Holmes Super Collection' into your Amazon search bar. Enjoy over 2 million words of MORE SHERLOCK.

www.SherlockHolmesMystery.com

The Adventure of the Resident Patient

The Original Sherlock Holmes Story

Arthur Conan Doyle

The Resident Patient

In glancing over the somewhat incoherent series of
memoirs with which I have endeavored to illustrate a few
of the mental peculiarities of my friend, Mr. Sherlock
Holmes, I have been struck by the difficulty which I have
experienced in picking out examples which shall in every way
answer my purpose. For in those cases in which Holmes has
performed some tour de force of analytical reasoning, and has
demonstrated the value of his peculiar methods of investigation,
the facts themselves have often been so slight or so
commonplace that I could not feel justified in laying them before
the public. On the other hand, it has frequently happened that
he has been concerned in some research where the facts have
been of the most remarkable and dramatic character, but where
the share which he has himself taken in determining their
causes has been less pronounced than I, as his biographer, could

wish. The small matter which I have chronicled under the heading of A Study in Scarlet, and that other later one connected with the loss of the Gloria Scott, may serve as examples of this Scylla and Charybdis which are forever threatening his historian. It may be that, in the business of which I am now about to write, the part which my friend played is not sufficiently accentuated and yet the whole train of circumstances is so remarkable that I cannot bring myself to omit it entirely from this series. I cannot be sure of the exact date, for some of my memoranda upon the matter have been mislaid, but it must have been towards the end of the first year during which Holmes and I shared chambers in Baker Street. It was boisterous October weather, and we had both remained indoors all day, I because I feared with my shaken health to face the keen autumn wind, while he was deep in some of those abstruse chemical investigations which absorbed him utterly as long as he was engaged upon them. Towards evening, however, the breaking of a test-tube brought his research to a premature ending, and he sprang up from his chair with an exclamation of impatience and a clouded brow.

"A day's work ruined, Watson," said he, striding across to the window. "Ha! The stars are out and the wind has fallen. What do you say to a ramble through London?"

I was weary of our little sitting-room and gladly acquiesced. For three hours we strolled about together, watching the ever-changing kaleidoscope of life as it ebbs and flows through Fleet Street and the Strand. His characteristic talk, with its keen observance of detail and subtle power of inference held me amused and enthralled. It was ten o'clock before we reached Baker Street again. A brougham was waiting at our door.

"Hum! A doctor's—general practitioner, I perceive," said Holmes. "Not been long in practice, but has had a good deal to do. Come to consult us, I fancy! Lucky we came back!"

I was sufficiently conversant with Holmes's methods to be able to follow his reasoning, and to see that the nature and state of the various medical instruments in the wicker basket which hung in the lamplight inside the brougham had given him the data for his swift deduction. The light in our window above showed that this late visit was indeed intended for us. With some curiosity as to what could have sent a brother medico to us at such an hour, I followed Holmes into our sanctum.

A pale, taper-faced man with sandy whiskers rose up from a chair by the fire as we entered. His age may not have been more than three or four and thirty, but his haggard expression and unhealthy hue told of a life which has sapped his strength and robbed him of his youth. His manner was nervous and shy, like that of a sensitive gentleman, and the thin white hand which he laid on the mantelpiece as he rose was that of an artist rather than of a surgeon. His dress was quiet and sombre—a black frock-coat, dark trousers, and a touch of color about his necktie.

"Good-evening, doctor," said Holmes, cheerily. "I am glad to see that you have only been waiting a very few minutes."

"You spoke to my coachman, then?"

"No, it was the candle on the side-table that told me. Pray resume your seat and let me know how I can serve you."

"My name is Doctor Percy Trevelyan," said our visitor, "and I live at 403 Brook Street."

"Are you not the author of a monograph upon obscure nervous lesions?" I asked.

His pale cheeks flushed with pleasure at hearing that his work was known to me.

"I so seldom hear of the work that I thought it was quite dead," said he. "My publishers gave me a most discouraging account of its sale. You are yourself, I presume, a medical man?"

"A retired army surgeon."

"My own hobby has always been nervous disease. I should wish to make it an absolute specialty, but, of course, a man must take what he can get at first. This, however, is beside the question, Mr. Sherlock Holmes, and I quite appreciate how valuable your time is. The fact is that a very singular train of events has occurred recently at my house in Brook Street, and to-night they came to such a head that I felt it was quite impossible for me to wait another hour before asking for your advice and assistance."

Sherlock Holmes sat down and lit his pipe. "You are very welcome to both," said he. "Pray let me have a detailed account of what the circumstances are which have disturbed you."

"One or two of them are so trivial," said Dr. Trevelyan, "that really I am almost ashamed to mention them. But the matter is so inexplicable, and the recent turn which it has taken is so elaborate, that I shall lay it all before you, and you shall judge what is essential and what is not.

"I am compelled, to begin with, to say something of my own college career. I am a London University man, you know, and I am sure that you will not think that I am unduly singing my own praises if I say that my student career was considered by my professors to be a very promising one. After I had graduated I continued to devote myself to research, occupying a minor position in King's College Hospital, and I was fortunate enough to excite considerable interest by my research into the pathology of catalepsy, and finally to win the Bruce Pinkerton prize and medal by the monograph on nervous lesions to which your friend has just alluded. I should not go too far if I were to say that there was a general impression at that time that a distinguished career lay before me.

"But the one great stumbling-block lay in my want of capital. As you will readily understand, a specialist who aims high is compelled to start in one of a dozen streets in the Cavendish Square quarter, all of which entail enormous rents and furnishing expenses. Besides this preliminary outlay, he must be prepared to keep himself for some years, and to hire a presentable carriage and horse. To do this was quite beyond my power, and I could only hope that by economy I might in ten years' time save enough to enable me to put up my plate. Suddenly, however, an unexpected incident opened up quite a new prospect to me.

"This was a visit from a gentleman of the name of Blessington, who was a complete stranger to me. He came up to my room one morning, and plunged into business in an instant.

"'You are the same Percy Trevelyan who has had so distinguished a career and won a great prize lately?' said he.

"I bowed.

"'Answer me frankly,' he continued, 'for you will find it to your interest to do so. You have all the cleverness which makes a successful man. Have you the tact?'

"I could not help smiling at the abruptness of the question.

"'I trust that I have my share,' I said.

"'Any bad habits? Not drawn towards drink, eh?'

"'Really, sir!' I cried.

"'Quite right! That's all right! But I was bound to ask. With all these qualities, why are you not in practice?'

"I shrugged my shoulders.

"'Come, come!' said he, in his bustling way. 'It's the old story. More in your brains than in your pocket, eh? What would you say if I were to start you in Brook Street?'

"I stared at him in astonishment.

"'Oh, it's for my sake, not for yours,' he cried. 'I'll be perfectly frank with you, and if it suits you it will suit me very well. I have a few thousands to invest, d'ye see, and I think I'll sink them in you.'

"'But why?' I gasped.

"'Well, it's just like any other speculation, and safer than most.'

"'What am I to do, then?'

"'I'll tell you. I'll take the house, furnish it, pay the maids, and run the whole place. All you have to do is just to wear out

130

your chair in the consulting-room. I'll let you have pocket-money and everything. Then you hand over to me three quarters of what you earn, and you keep the other quarter for yourself.'

"This was the strange proposal, Mr. Holmes, with which the man Blessington approached me. I won't weary you with the account of how we bargained and negotiated. It ended in my moving into the house next Lady-day, and starting in practice on very much the same conditions as he had suggested. He came himself to live with me in the character of a resident patient. His heart was weak, it appears, and he needed constant medical supervision. He turned the two best rooms of the first floor into a sitting-room and bedroom for himself. He was a man of singular habits, shunning company and very seldom going out. His life was irregular, but in one respect he was regularity itself. Every evening, at the same hour, he walked into the consulting-room, examined the books, put down five and three-pence for every guinea that I had earned, and carried the rest off to the strong-box in his own room.

"I may say with confidence that he never had occasion to regret his speculation. From the first it was a success. A few good cases and the reputation which I had won in the hospital brought me rapidly to the front, and during the last few years I have made him a rich man.

"So much, Mr. Holmes, for my past history and my relations with Mr. Blessington. It only remains for me now to tell you what has occurred to bring me here to-night.

"Some weeks ago Mr. Blessington came down to me in, as it seemed to me, a state of considerable agitation. He spoke of some burglary which, he said, had been committed in the West End, and he appeared, I remember, to be quite unnecessarily excited about it, declaring that a day should not pass before we should add stronger bolts to our windows and doors. For a week he continued to be in a peculiar state of restlessness, peering continually out of the windows, and ceasing to take the short walk which had usually been the prelude to his dinner. From his manner it struck me that he was in mortal dread of something or somebody, but when I questioned him upon the point he became so offensive that I was compelled to drop the subject. Gradually, as time passed, his fears appeared to die away, and he had renewed his former habits, when a fresh event reduced him to the pitiable state of prostration in which he now lies.

"What happened was this. Two days ago I received the letter which I now read to you. Neither address nor date is attached to it.

"'A Russian nobleman who is now resident in England,' it runs, 'would be glad to avail himself of the professional assistance of Dr. Percy Trevelyan. He has been for some years a victim to cataleptic attacks, on which, as is well known, Dr. Trevelyan is an authority. He proposes to call at about quarter past six to-morrow evening, if Dr. Trevelyan will make it convenient to be at home.'

"This letter interested me deeply, because the chief difficulty in the study of catalepsy is the rareness of the disease. You may believe, then, that I was in my consulting-room when, at the appointed hour, the page showed in the patient.

"He was an elderly man, thin, demure, and commonplace—by no means the conception one forms of a Russian nobleman. I was much more struck by the appearance of his companion. This was a tall young man, surprisingly handsome, with a dark, fierce face, and the limbs and chest of a Hercules. He had his hand under the other's arm as they entered, and helped him to a chair with a tenderness which one would hardly have expected from his appearance.

"'You will excuse my coming in, doctor,' said he to me, speaking English with a slight lisp. 'This is my father, and his health is a matter of the most overwhelming importance to me.'

"I was touched by this filial anxiety. 'You would, perhaps, care to remain during the consultation?' said I.

"'Not for the world,' he cried with a gesture of horror. 'It is more painful to me than I can express. If I were to see my father in one of these dreadful seizures I am convinced that I should never survive it. My own nervous system is an exceptionally sensitive one. With your permission, I will remain in the waiting-room while you go into my father's case.'

"To this, of course, I assented, and the young man withdrew. The patient and I then plunged into a discussion of his case, of which I took exhaustive notes. He was not remarkable for intelligence, and his answers were frequently obscure, which I attributed to his limited acquaintance with our language. Suddenly, however, as I sat writing, he ceased to give any answer at all to my inquiries, and on my turning towards him I was shocked to see that he was sitting bolt upright in his chair, staring at me with a perfectly blank and rigid face. He was again in the grip of his mysterious malady.

"My first feeling, as I have just said, was one of pity and horror. My second, I fear, was rather one of professional satisfaction. I made notes of my patient's pulse and temperature, tested the rigidity of his muscles, and examined his reflexes. There was nothing markedly abnormal in any of these conditions, which harmonized with my former experiences. I had obtained good results in such cases by the inhalation of nitrite of amyl, and the present seemed an admirable opportunity of testing its virtues. The bottle was downstairs in my laboratory, so leaving my patient seated in his chair, I ran down to get it. There was some little delay in finding it—five minutes, let us say—and then I returned. Imagine my amazement to find the room empty and the patient gone.

"Of course, my first act was to run into the waiting-room. The son had gone also. The hall door had been closed, but not shut. My page who admits patients is a new boy and by no means quick. He waits downstairs, and runs up to show patients out when I ring the consulting-room bell. He had heard nothing, and the affair remained a complete mystery. Mr. Blessington came in from his walk shortly afterwards, but I did not say anything to him upon the subject, for, to tell the truth, I have got in the way of late of holding as little communication with him as possible.

"Well, I never thought that I should see anything more of the Russian and his son, so you can imagine my amazement when, at the very same hour this evening, they both came marching into my consulting-room, just as they had done before.

"'I feel that I owe you a great many apologies for my abrupt departure yesterday, doctor,' said my patient.

"'I confess that I was very much surprised at it,' said I.

"'Well, the fact is,' he remarked, 'that when I recover from these attacks my mind is always very clouded as to all that has gone before. I woke up in a strange room, as it seemed to me, and made my way out into the street in a sort of dazed way when you were absent.' Holmes and Watson help an elderly man into a chair

"'And I,' said the son, 'seeing my father pass the door of the waiting-room, naturally thought that the consultation had come to an end. It was not until we had reached home that I began to realize the true state of affairs.'

"'Well,' said I, laughing, 'there is no harm done except that you puzzled me terribly; so if you, sir, would kindly step into the waiting-room I shall be happy to continue our consultation which was brought to so abrupt an ending.'

"'For half an hour or so I discussed that old gentleman's symptoms with him, and then, having prescribed for him, I saw him go off upon the arm of his son.

"I have told you that Mr. Blessington generally chose this hour of the day for his exercise. He came in shortly afterwards and passed upstairs. An instant later I heard him running down, and he burst into my consulting-room like a man who is mad with panic.

"'Who has been in my room?' he cried.

"'No one,' said I.

"'It's a lie! He yelled. 'Come up and look!'

"I passed over the grossness of his language, as he seemed half out of his mind with fear. When I went upstairs with him he pointed to several footprints upon the light carpet.

"'D'you mean to say those are mine?' he cried.

"They were certainly very much larger than any which he could have made, and were evidently quite fresh. It rained hard this afternoon, as you know, and my patients were the only people who called. It must have been the case, then, that the man in the waiting-room had, for some reason, while I was busy with the other, ascended to the room of my resident patient. Nothing had been touched or taken, but there were the footprints to prove that the intrusion was an undoubted fact.

"Mr. Blessington seemed more excited over the matter than I should have thought possible, though of course it was enough to disturb anybody's peace of mind. He actually sat crying in an arm-chair, and I could hardly get him to speak coherently. It was his suggestion that I should come round to you, and of course I at once saw the propriety of it, for certainly the incident is a very singular one, though he appears to completely overrate its importance. If you would only come back with me in my brougham, you would at least be able to soothe him, though I can hardly hope that you will be able to explain this remarkable occurrence."

Sherlock Holmes had listened to this long narrative with an intentness which showed me that his interest was keenly aroused. His face was as impassive as ever, but his lids had drooped more heavily over his eyes, and his smoke had curled up more thickly from his pipe to emphasize each curious episode in the doctor's tale. As our visitor concluded, Holmes sprang up without a word, handed me my hat, picked his own from the table, and followed Dr. Trevelyan to the door. Within a quarter of an hour we had been dropped at the door of the physician's residence in Brook Street, one of those sombre, flat-faced houses which one associates with a West-End practice. A small page admitted us, and we began at once to ascend the broad, well-carpeted stair.

But a singular interruption brought us to a standstill. The light at the top was suddenly whisked out, and from the darkness came a reedy, quivering voice.

"I have a pistol," it cried. "I give you my word that I'll fire if you come any nearer."

"This really grows outrageous, Mr. Blessington," cried Dr. Trevelyan.

"Oh, then it is you, doctor," said the voice, with a great heave of relief. "But those other gentlemen, are they what they pretend to be?"

We were conscious of a long scrutiny out of the darkness.

"Yes, yes, it's all right," said the voice at last. "You can come up, and I am sorry if my precautions have annoyed you."

He relit the stair gas as he spoke, and we saw before us a singular-looking man, whose appearance, as well as his voice, testified to his jangled nerves. He was very fat, but had apparently at some time been much fatter, so that the skin hung about his face in loose pouches, like the cheeks of a blood-hound. He was of a sickly color, and his thin, sandy hair seemed to bristle up with the intensity of his emotion. In his hand he held a pistol, but he thrust it into his pocket as we advanced.

"Good-evening, Mr. Holmes," said he. "I am sure I am very much obliged to you for coming round. No one ever needed your advice more than I do. I suppose that Dr. Trevelyan has told you of this most unwarrantable intrusion into my rooms."

"Quite so," said Holmes. "Who are these two men Mr. Blessington, and why do they wish to molest you?"

"Well, well," said the resident patient, in a nervous fashion, "of course it is hard to say that. You can hardly expect me to answer that, Mr. Holmes."

"Do you mean that you don't know?"

"Come in here, if you please. Just have the kindness to step in here."

He led the way into his bedroom, which was large and comfortably furnished.

"You see that," said he, pointing to a big black box at the end of his bed. "I have never been a very rich man, Mr. Holmes—never made but one investment in my life, as Dr. Trevelyan would tell you. But I don't believe in bankers. I would never trust a banker, Mr. Holmes. Between ourselves, what little I have is in that box, so you can understand what it means to me when people force themselves into my rooms."

Holmes looked at Blessington in his questioning way and shook his head.

"I cannot possibly advise you if you try to deceive me," said he.

"But I have told you everything."

Holmes turned on his heel with a gesture of disgust. "Good-night, Dr. Trevelyan," said he.

"And no advice for me?" cried Blessington, in a breaking voice.

"My advice to your, sir, is to speak the truth."

A minute later we were in the street and walking for home. We had crossed Oxford Street and were half way down Harley Street before I could get a word from my companion.

"Sorry to bring you out on such a fool's errand, Watson," he said at last. "It is an interesting case, too, at the bottom of it."

"I can make little of it," I confessed.

"Well, it is quite evident that there are two men—more, perhaps, but at least two—who are determined for some reason to get at this fellow Blessington. I have no doubt in my mind that both on the first and on the second occasion that young man penetrated to Blessington's room, while his confederate, by an ingenious device, kept the doctor from interfering."

"And the catalepsy?"

"A fraudulent imitation, Watson, though I should hardly dare to hint as much to our specialist. It is a very easy complaint to imitate. I have done it myself."

"And then?"

"By the purest chance Blessington was out on each occasion. Their reason for choosing so unusual an hour for a consultation was obviously to insure that there should be no other patient in the waiting-room. It just happened, however, that this hour coincided with Blessington's constitutional, which seems to show that they were not very well acquainted with his daily routine. Of course, if they had been merely after plunder they would at least have made some attempt to search for it. Besides, I can read in a man's eye when it is his own skin that he is frightened for. It is inconceivable that this fellow could have made two such vindictive enemies as these appear to be without knowing of it. I hold it, therefore, to be certain that he does know who these men are, and that for reasons of his own he suppresses it. It is just possible that to-morrow may find him in a more communicative mood."

"Is there not one alternative," I suggested, "grotesquely improbably, no doubt, but still just conceivable? Might the whole story of the cataleptic Russian and his son be a concoction of Dr. Trevelyan's, who has, for his own purposes, been in Blessington's rooms?"

I saw in the gaslight that Holmes wore an amused smile at this brilliant departure of mine.

"My dear fellow," said he, "it was one of the first solutions which occurred to me, but I was soon able to corroborate the doctor's tale. This young man has left prints upon the stair-carpet which made it quite superfluous for me to ask to see those which he had made in the room. When I tell you that his shoes were square-toed instead of being pointed like Blessington's, and were quite an inch and a third longer than the doctor's, you will acknowledge that there can be no doubt as to his individuality. But we may sleep on it now, for I shall be surprised if we do not hear something further from Brook Street in the morning."

Sherlock Holmes's prophecy was soon fulfilled, and in a dramatic fashion. At half-past seven next morning, in the first glimmer of daylight, I found him standing by my bedside in his dressing-gown.

"There's a brougham waiting for us, Watson," said he.

"What's the matter, then?"

"The Brook Street business."

"Any fresh news?"

"Tragic, but ambiguous," said he, pulling up the blind. "Look at this—a sheet from a note-book, with 'For God's sake come at once—P. T.,' scrawled upon it in pencil. Our friend, the doctor, was hard put to it when he wrote this. Come along, my dear fellow, for it's an urgent call."

In a quarter of an hour or so we were back at the physician's house. He came running out to meet us with a face of horror.

"Oh, such a business!" he cried, with his hands to his temples.

"What then?"

"Blessington has committed suicide!"

Holmes whistled.

"Yes, he hanged himself during the night."

We had entered, and the doctor had preceded us into what was evidently his waiting-room.

"I really hardly know what I am doing," he cried. "The police are already upstairs. It has shaken me most dreadfully."

"When did you find it out?"

"He has a cup of tea taken in to him early every morning. When the maid entered, about seven, there the unfortunate

141

fellow was hanging in the middle of the room. He had tied his cord to the hook on which the heavy lamp used to hang, and he had jumped off from the top of the very box that he showed us yesterday."

Holmes stood for a moment in deep thought.

"With your permission," said he at last, "I should like to go upstairs and look into the matter."

We both ascended, followed by the doctor.

It was a dreadful sight which met us as we entered the bedroom door. I have spoken of the impression of flabbiness which this man Blessington conveyed. As he dangled from the hook it was exaggerated and intensified until he was scarce human in his appearance. The neck was drawn out like a plucked chicken's, making the rest of him seem the more obese and unnatural by the contrast. He was clad only in his long night-dress, and his swollen ankles and ungainly feet protruded starkly from beneath it. Beside him stood a smart-looking police-inspector, who was taking notes in a pocket-book.

"Ah, Mr. Holmes," said he, heartily, as my friend entered, "I am delighted to see you."

"Good-morning, Lanner," answered Holmes; "you won't think me an intruder, I am sure. Have you heard of the events which led up to this affair?"

"Yes, I heard something of them."

"Have you formed any opinion?"

"As far as I can see, the man has been driven out of his senses by fright. The bed has been well slept in, you see. There's his impression deep enough. It's about five in the morning, you know, that suicides are most common. That would be about his time for hanging himself. It seems to have been a very deliberate affair."

"I should say that he has been dead about three hours, judging by the rigidity of the muscles," said I.

"Noticed anything peculiar about the room?" asked Holmes.

"Found a screw-driver and some screws on the wash-hand stand. Seems to have smoked heavily during the night, too. Here are four cigar-ends that I picked out of the fireplace."

"Hum!" said Holmes, "have you got his cigar-holder?"

"No, I have seen none."

"His cigar-case, then?"

"Yes, it was in his coat-pocket."

Holmes opened it and smelled the single cigar which it contained.

"Oh, this is an Havana, and these others are cigars of the peculiar sort which are imported by the Dutch from their East Indian colonies. They are usually wrapped in straw, you know, and are thinner for their length than any other brand." He picked up the four ends and examined them with his pocket-lens.

"Two of these have been smoked from a holder and two without," said he. "Two have been cut by a not very sharp knife, and two have had the ends bitten off by a set of excellent teeth. This is no suicide, Mr. Lanner. It is a very deeply planned and cold-blooded murder."

"Impossible!" cried the inspector.

"And why?"

"Why should any one murder a man in so clumsy a fashion as by hanging him?"

"That is what we have to find out."

"How could they get in?"

"Through the front door."

"It was barred in the morning."

"Then it was barred after them."

"How do you know?"

"I saw their traces. Excuse me a moment, and I may be able to give you some further information about it."

He went over to the door, and turning the lock he examined it in his methodical way. Then he took out the key, which was on the inside, and inspected that also. The bed, the carpet, the chairs the mantelpiece, the dead body, and the rope were each in turn examined, until at last he professed himself satisfied, and with my aid and that of the inspector cut down the wretched object and laid it reverently under a sheet.

"How about this rope?" he asked.

"It is cut off this," said Dr. Trevelyan, drawing a large coil from under the bed. "He was morbidly nervous of fire, and always kept this beside him, so that he might escape by the window in case the stairs were burning."

"That must have saved them trouble," said Holmes, thoughtfully. "Yes, the actual facts are very plain, and I shall be surprised if by the afternoon I cannot give you the reasons for them as well. I will take this photograph of Blessington, which I see upon the mantelpiece, as it may help me in my inquiries."

"But you have told us nothing!" cried the doctor.

"Oh, there can be no doubt as to the sequence of events," said Holmes. "There were three of them in it: the young man, the old man, and a third, to whose identity I have no clue. The first two, I need hardly remark, are the same who masqueraded as the Russian count and his son, so we can give a very full description of them. They were admitted by a confederate inside the house. If I might offer you a word of advice, Inspector, it would be to arrest the page, who, as I understand, has only recently come into your service, Doctor."

"The young imp cannot be found," said Dr. Trevelyan; "the maid and the cook have just been searching for him."

Holmes shrugged his shoulders.

"He has played a not unimportant part in this drama," said he. "The three men having ascended the stairs, which they did on tiptoe, the elder man first, the younger man second, and the man in the rear—"

"My dear Holmes!" I ejaculated.

"Oh, there could be no question as to the superimposing of the footmarks. I had the advantage of learning which was which last night. They ascended, then, to Mr. Blessington's room, the door of which they found to be locked. With the help of a wire, however, they forced round the key. Even without the lens you will perceive, by the scratches on this ward, where the pressure was applied.

"On entering the room their first proceeding must have been to gag Mr. Blessington. He may have been asleep, or he may have been so paralyzed with terror as to have been unable to cry out. These walls are thick, and it is conceivable that his shriek, if he had time to utter one, was unheard.

"Having secured him, it is evident to me that a consultation of some sort was held. Probably it was something in the nature of a judicial proceeding. It must have lasted for some time, for it was then that these cigars were smoked. The older man sat in that wicker chair; it was he who used the cigar-holder. The younger man sat over yonder; he knocked his ash off against the chest of drawers. The third fellow paced up and down. Blessington, I think, sat upright in the bed, but of that I cannot be absolutely certain.

"Well, it ended by their taking Blessington and hanging him. The matter was so prearranged that it is my belief that they brought with them some sort of block or pulley which might serve as a gallows. That screw-driver and those screws were, as I conceive, for fixing it up. Seeing the hook, however they naturally saved themselves the trouble. Having finished their work they made off, and the door was barred behind them by their confederate."

We had all listened with the deepest interest to this sketch of the night's doings, which Holmes had deduced from signs so subtle and minute that, even when he had pointed them out to us, we could scarcely follow him in his reasoning. The inspector hurried away on the instant to make inquiries about the page, while Holmes and I returned to Baker Street for breakfast.

"I'll be back by three," said he, when we had finished our meal. "Both the inspector and the doctor will meet me here at that hour, and I hope by that time to have cleared up any little obscurity which the case may still present."

Our visitors arrived at the appointed time, but it was a quarter to four before my friend put in an appearance. From his expression as he entered, however, I could see that all had gone well with him.

"Any news, Inspector?"

"We have got the boy, sir."

"Excellent, and I have got the men."

"You have got them!" we cried, all three.

"Well, at least I have got their identity. This so-called Blessington is, as I expected, well known at headquarters, and so are his assailants. Their names are Biddle, Hayward, and Moffat."

"The Worthingdon bank gang," cried the inspector.

"Precisely," said Holmes.

"Then Blessington must have been Sutton."

"Exactly," said Holmes.

"Why, that makes it as clear as crystal," said the inspector.

But Trevelyan and I looked at each other in bewilderment.

"You must surely remember the great Worthingdon bank business," said Holmes. "Five men were in it—these four and a fifth called Cartwright. Tobin, the care-taker, was murdered, and the thieves got away with seven thousand pounds. This was in 1875. They were all five arrested, but the evidence against them was by no means conclusive. This Blessington or Sutton, who was the worst of the gang, turned informer. On his evidence Cartwright was hanged and the other three got fifteen years apiece. When they got out the other day, which was some years before their full term, they set themselves, as you perceive, to hunt down the traitor and to avenge the death of their comrade upon him. Twice they tried to get at him and failed; a third time, you see, it came off. Is there anything further which I can explain, Dr. Trevelyan?"

"I think you have made it all remarkable clear," said the doctor. "No doubt the day on which he was perturbed was the day when he had seen of their release in the newspapers."

"Quite so. His talk about a burglary was the merest blind."

"But why could he not tell you this?"

"Well, my dear sir, knowing the vindictive character of his old associates, he was trying to hide his own identity from everybody as long as he could. His secret was a shameful one, and he could not bring himself to divulge it. However, wretch as he was, he was still living under the shield of British law, and I have no doubt, Inspector, that you will see that, though that shield may fail to guard, the sword of justice is still there to avenge."

Such were the singular circumstances in connection with the Resident Patient and the Brook Street Doctor. From that night nothing has been seen of the three murderers by the police, and it is surmised at Scotland Yard that they were among the passengers of the ill-fated steamer Norah Creina, which was lost some years ago with all hands upon the Portuguese coast, some leagues to the north of Oporto. The proceedings against the page broke down for want of evidence, and the Brook Street Mystery, as it was called, has never until now been fully dealt with in any public print.

Note to the Reader:

The above text of the Canonical story, *The Adventure of the Resident Patient*, is as it originally appeared in the *Strand* magazine. In later editions, the introductory paragraphs were altered and several paragraphs that had been written for the story *The Cardboard Box* were inserted. This later version appears in many printings of this story, especially those published in the United States.

Made in United States
Orlando, FL
28 May 2024

47277837R00095